Summer Silver

OLIVER & BOYD

Summer Silver

ERIC HOUGHTON

Illustrated by
SHIRLEY HUGHES

Oliver and Boyd Ltd
Tweeddale Court, Edinburgh 1
39a Welbeck Street, London W.1

Printed in Great Britain by
Morrison and Gibb Limited, London and Edinburgh

Contents

FACTORIES

FACTORIES

FACTORIES

Boultons

OLD FIELD

River Thorpe

Running-tents

OLD VILLAGE

St. Mary's Church

Vicarage

COUNCIL ESTATE

SHOPS

High St

Recreation Park

Town Hall

SHOPS

High Street

Sutcliff St

School

Barnsley Rd

High Street

River Thorpe

Bravender Pl

ROSEDALE HOUSING ESTATE

Station

RAILS DEPOT

N W S E

1

The Hidden Field

The hole in the fence was no more than twelve inches wide, but Colin had wriggled through slimmer gaps than that. He glanced swiftly up and down the street. The two women he had passed three minutes ago were still gossiping on the corner where the houses ended; ahead it was empty except for a couple of lorries swinging into one of the factories—all new, high-walled buildings that crowded the pavements for as far as he could see, matching the drab six-foot fence beside him.

The women seemed to be separating; the one with the pram was manoeuvring it through the gateway of the last house. Better wait until they had gone properly. Colin pretended to be interested in the 'For Sale' board fixed to the fence. Judging by its condition, whatever lay behind the patchwork of corrugated iron and mouldering boards had lain unwanted for many years.

The women made off—one indoors, the other down the street towards the shopping-centre. It was the work of an instant to thrust his left foot through the hole, duck his head beneath the jagged iron and twist smartly inside, taking care that his coat pocket, bulging with his pencil-case and sketch-book, did not snag on the sides.

And there he was, in a different, more comforting
world.

A jungle of plants and bushes lay before him. The
ground was humped and broken into banks, ditches
and hollows—Colin could not help thinking of a heavy
sea that had somehow frozen. Shut in on two sides by
the fence, on the other two by the high, red-brick walls
of factory yards, the wilderness appeared to be almost
as large as a football field. Twenty yards away, at the
near end of a ridge, stood the leafless willow tree whose

topmost boughs he had spotted with homesick eagerness from the street.

Grasping the pencil-case tightly in his pocket, Colin hurried over the wet grass, drinking in its pleasant, familiar scent.

The ridge appeared to be the ideal position ; its long crest, as straight as if shaped by man, was high enough to give a good view of almost three-quarters of the field. Huddling down against the willow trunk, out of the February wind, Colin pulled out his sketch-book and began to draw.

The book was merely a pocket-sized pad, the latest of many which he was forever buying and filling with quick sketches. His pencil-case, however—holding a dozen crayons, a rubber and nine-inch ruler in separate compartments—had lasted many years ; it had been a birthday present from his parents, and had become as much a part of him as the hand which held his pencil.

Ever since he had started school, drawing had fascinated him. Beginning with sketching from his imagination, making his pencil set down whatever pictures his mind conjured up, he had gradually progressed to drawing from real life : houses, dogs, trees, tractors—anything that stayed still long enough for him to tug out his pad and crayons. Over the last two or three years he had become able to set down a good likeness within ten minutes.

His skill with the brush, however, lagged well behind his pencil-work ; it was garish and crude, and he knew he had spoilt dozens of neat sketches by trying to paint in the colours instead of crayoning. In fact since Christmas he had become so disgusted with his efforts that he had been trying to summon enough courage to ask his class-teacher for a few hints. Then last weekend had come their sudden upheaval, burying for good all his hopes in that direction, along with everything else he had lost at the same time.

He slid the pencil back into its compartment, and grimaced at the completed picture.

It was not quite right. The hawthorn trees looked real enough, as did the stream glittering in the foreground, but there was something unbalanced about the sketch as a whole. His eyes clouded with concentration.

The skyline : that was it, he decided. The tall buildings in the distance, beyond the modern, single-storey factories, were clustered on the left side of his picture, while there was an unsettling emptiness on the right. In fact the two tallest, the church spire and the sharp-peaked roof of what seemed an old mill, were almost in line with each other.

Determined to do better, he looked around for another position. It would have to be somewhere to the side, so that the spire and the high roof no longer clashed.

Over to the right, well past the hole in the fence where he had entered, was a small hillock. It wasn't as high as the ridge, but neither was anywhere else on the field. He pushed himself to his feet and set off, carefully clutching his book and pencil-case.

He had to leap the brook, and skirt several brambles,

before its grassy bank rose gently in front of him. Gathering his breath, he sprinted to the top.

That was better. The big buildings on the horizon were farther apart ; the background would look well balanced from here. Sitting down with his back and upturned collar to the wind, he began a fresh page in his sketch-book.

He was struggling to capture the correct shape of the steeple's weather-vane, when he heard a slight sound close behind him. With a start, he looked round.

He was no longer the only person in the field. A ginger-haired boy about his own age was standing behind, grinning down at him. There was something familiar about his clothes and chubby face, but it was not until he spoke that Colin recognized him.

'For a new boy, Trant, you get around pretty smartly, don't you ? How did you come to turn up here—follow your countryman's nose ? '

'Just luck,' grunted Colin, ignoring the sneer. He remembered him now : Victor Brooksbank, one of the boys in the back row of his new class. ' I thought I'd do some exploring in this direction, and happened to spot that gap in the fence.' With an effort he managed to keep the disappointment out of his voice ; he should have known a place like this was too good to be found only by him—the school wasn't above half a mile away.

' What d'you think of Wheatleigh after your first week here, then ? ' demanded Brooksbank, grinning. ' Like it better than living in a one-horse village, I bet ! '

'Oh, Cullerton was all right,' muttered Colin guardedly. 'Plenty of woods and commons, like this——'

'Any cinemas there?' interrupted Brooksbank tersely, squatting down beside him.

'Not in the village itself,' admitted Colin. 'Just half an hour on the bus—in the next town.'

'Sounds like a graveyard,' sniffed the other. 'We've got four here, you know. Swimming-baths and a roller-drome too. You skate?'

'Never had the chance to learn,' murmured Colin. He put his pencil back in the case beside him on the grass, and eased the book on his knee; better forget about drawing till the other had gone.

'You get yourself some skates,' advised Brooksbank grandly. 'You'll soon pick it up in our playground; Old Hully—that's the Head—made a rule stopping it, but we do it when he's gone, after four. You keen on drawing, then? Let's have a look, will you?'

He lifted the sketch-book from Colin's knee, and began to flick through its pages. He barely glanced at the meticulous drawing of their old cottage in Cullerton; it had been Colin's labour of love on their last day there.

'Mmm—not bad, I suppose,' concluded Brooksbank, jerking back his ginger hair. He flicked the book back on to Colin's knee. 'Miss Seymour might do you a favour one day, and pin one on the classroom wall.'

With a grunt he straightened himself up, and started to work some life back into his cramped legs. Colin

12

remembered dryly that whoever had had his picture pinned up after Thursday's Art period, it certainly hadn't been Brooksbank.

'Blow me—look at the time!' blurted the other suddenly. The church clock in the distance said half past eleven. 'I'll be late for dinner. S'long. See you at school on Monday. Don't forget about the skates.'

Colin watched him hurry down the bank and race past the brambles. Who wants four cinemas? he thought grimly; you can't visit more than one at a time.

Brooksbank disappeared at full pelt towards the fence, and Colin turned back to his sketch.

He would have one more try at the weather-vane—and then what? That tall factory didn't look too convincing, more like a giant dolls' house; he'd touch that up afterwards. Gazing critically at the spire once more, he groped beside him for the pencil-case.

His fingers met nothing but damp grass. He looked down impatiently. It wasn't there. Sighing at his own stupidity, he turned to the other side. It wasn't there either.

Kneeling down, he began to feel about in the tangled grasses and weeds. There were any number of promising lumps buried among the dead stems, but they turned out to be stones or bits of broken bottle. He even unearthed an old briar-pipe and a lid like the top of his money-box, bearing the letters C.N.K. He pushed these two finds in his pocket, and widened his search.

13

After five minutes he was convinced the case was nowhere near where he had been sitting. With a frown of puzzlement he moved farther down the bank : maybe Brooksbank's dashing-off had sent it flying . . .

Brooksbank !

Colin's cheeks darkened. He sprinted down the hillock and made for the hole in the fence. Only when he had squirmed through on to the pavement did he realize how futile it was. For one thing, he was far too late. And for another, Brooksbank could have taken any one of half a dozen turnings, very likely knowing his way through that drab maze of streets as easily as Colin had known every track through Cullerton woods.

2

Settling In

Colin decided against saying anything at home about what had happened that Saturday. There was a chance he'd be able to get it back at school the next week; as a rule, he didn't like telling tales, but his pencil-case was something special and made things different.

The worst part was that it would be just his word against Brooksbank's; and if the case had been taken deliberately, he might as well say goodbye to it now —unless Brooksbank was fool enough to bring it to school. Of course, there was always the chance that it had been picked up absent-mindedly, rather in the way his dad kept pocketing and bringing home from work quite useless bolts and screws. And if that was what had happened, it was possible Brooksbank would find it over the weekend and have it ready for him on Monday morning.

Quite a doubtful 'if', Colin told himself grimly. Still, he would just have to wait and see. He *might* get it back without his mother or father knowing it had ever gone, unless they were sharp enough to notice its absence during Sunday.

As things turned out, both his parents were far too busy. They had had to move into Wheatleigh so suddenly that Mrs Trant had been able to do no more than sweep the worst of the rubbish from the rooms before their furniture descended on them from Cullerton. With her husband home from work to help, Sunday had accordingly been earmarked as Scrubbing-from-Top-to-Bottom Day, for she found it impossible to relax till she knew everything had been thoroughly washed and disinfected.

'It's so filthy you can almost *smell* the germs and damp,' she declared over an early breakfast that Sunday. ' A good spring-clean's what it wants and a good spring-clean is what it's going to get, before I'm a day older.'

Throughout that morning the two men of the house found themselves very busy indeed, moving wardrobes, beds and sideboards, rolling up rugs and carpets, and carrying buckets of warm water all over the house. And when dinner came—rather late and lukewarm—most of the heavy work was conquered.

' As you won't be wanting to move things back till the floors have aired a bit,' smiled Mr Trant, setting down his last cup of tea, ' Colin and I might as well start *our* spot of spring-cleaning. Come on, son.'

Colin laid down his library book, relieved there was to be no more bucket-duty ; he had a fairly shrewd idea of what his father had in mind.

Nine-month-old Tim, Colin's brother, was lying in his pram in the backyard. Mr Trant peeped in, smiled, and began to rock it gently.

' That's the enemy, Colin,' he murmured, nodding towards the old greenhouse beside the gate.

If any further proof were needed, after seeing the original state of the rooms, that whoever had lived here before them had certainly been no handyman, one look at the greenhouse was enough. The door hung dangerously from one hinge, with its two bottom panels rotted away ; the rest of the woodwork looked almost as bad, without a single flake of paint left on it ; the low brick walls sorely needed pointing, while Colin estimated it would take a van-load of glass to replace the panes that were smashed, split or simply non-existent.

'Going to patch it up into a toolshed, Dad ? ' he asked innocently.

Mr Trant grinned.

'No. We're going to take it to pieces. Most of it's only fit for the scrap-heap, but the bricks'll come in useful : later on we're going to build a conservatory over our back door.' He nodded towards the doorway behind them, where Mrs Trant was impatiently shaking out a duster.

It took Colin a moment or two before he remembered that the house next door had had one, back in Cullerton —a wide, glass porchway with its own door.

'As big as Mr Baxter's ? ' he asked keenly.

'Probably bigger,' replied his father with a smile. 'This place is nowhere near the size of our rambling great cottage, and your mum could well do with a bit more room. For one thing, we'll need somewhere for Tim's pram when it's raining.'

Colin could tell from the way his father was eyeing

the greenhouse that the details of their 'spring-cleaning' were already being worked out in his mind. Number 81 Sutcliff Street had fallen into very capable hands, he realized with a grin, for who better to restore it to rights than the railway-yard's new carpenter?

The next hour was both pleasant and hectic; and by the end of it, all that was left of the greenhouse was its waist-high brick wall. The dustbin was overflowing with rusty screws, splintered timber and broken glass, and beside it lay the roll of roofing-felt they had ripped off at the very beginning, and tied round with string for easier taking-away.

'You can have that—if it's any good to you,' grunted Mr Trant, wiping a hand across his sweating brow.

Colin shook his head regretfully. Wheatleigh had no secluded woods or dells like Cullerton, where a hide-out could be built and safely left for weeks on end . . . or had it?

'No?' continued his father. 'Anyway, there it is if you want it: you've earned it—what with helping your mum this morning, as well. You should be quite an expert at spring-cleaning by now!'

Colin grinned absently; of course, he knew the place wasn't as cut-off as he had first thought, but it would be worth a try.

'Need me any more, Dad?' he asked suddenly, hitching himself off the greenhouse wall, and shouldering the roofing-felt.

'No thanks, son,' declared Mr Trant. 'Going exploring again, eh? Well, wash all that muck off your

18

hands and face before you go. And get back by half past five, or else ! '

It was one of those winter days that are strangely exhilarating. The sun had turned the sky into a watery blue, a foretaste of spring that made you forget the cold. Reaching the end of Sutcliff Street, Colin turned his back on the now familiar road to school, and plunged into the criss-cross of side-streets.

Since the war, Wheatleigh, like other southern towns, had received a good sprinkling of new factories. Most of them made electrical or engineering goods, and had been built on the town outskirts, either bordering the river Thorpe or lining the railway track. It was these new industries which had steadily brought more and more goods-trains into town, making the railway depot so busy that over the past nine years the railway staff had been trebled. Colin's father was only one of many others whom the growing town had pulled in.

Most of the newcomers lived in rows of square, semi-detached council houses that were planted like a protecting maze between the factories and the town's shopping-centre ; and it was through this labyrinth that Colin was heading—greatly amused by the number of boiler-suits swinging from the clothes-lines, like flags of trade.

By the time he reached the end of the estate and the beginning of the fence, he had counted seventeen of them, for the sunshine had drawn the washing out of doors as a magnet pulls pins. Perhaps for the same

reason, there were more people about this time; fortunately, most of them were going in the opposite direction; they were probably only too glad to avoid the gaunt factories on a Sunday, Colin realized.

Pushing the felt in first, he squeezed smartly through the hole in the corrugated iron, fairly certain no one was looking.

Everything was just as before. In fact, it appeared snugger and greener, now wind had given place to sun. The humps of bare gorse and bramble looked like great sleepy hedgehogs on the slopes, while the grass was somehow stiffer and more sprightly. The whole field lay invitingly still and silent.

Colin ran eagerly to the high ridge and gazed around carefully from beneath the spider-leg boughs of the willow. There was nobody in sight. He wondered whether Brooksbank would appear again; in some ways that would be quite convenient. Shouldering his burden once more, he left the ridge, passed the hillock where last time he had finally settled to sketch, and set off across the field.

It was strangely satisfying to feel grass sinking crisply beneath his shoes once more; to sprint up hummocks with exactly enough speed to bring him comfortably to their crest; and to be able to poise himself for keenly judged leaps across ditches and over the low, leafless shrubs. This was the world he enjoyed, not the red-brick desert outside the fence.

Pausing where the ground shelved abruptly into a steep clay slope, he took stock. There were more trees at this lower end of the field, elders and hazels, but they were all rather stunted and scattered—not offering enough cover. Only after a minute or two did he notice an unobtrusive clump of hawthorns in one corner which looked more promising. Slithering down the greasy slope, he struck out in that direction.

The nearer he got to them, however, the more he found that the going was not as easy as it had seemed from above. Several times he stumbled over large square stones hidden beneath the tangled weeds and turf, and at others he had to negotiate jagged ridges of stonework embedded in the ground. They reminded him of the remains of ruined barns and stables you occasionally found in the country.

It was several minutes before he could make his way round the hawthorn thicket, keeping well clear of its black, spiky twigs. As he had calculated, it screened off almost completely one corner of the wasteland ; not twelve yards away the two boundary walls converged, and in between was the usual sprawl of humps and gullies. One of the deepest hollows lay in the immediate shelter of the trees, and the moment he saw it Colin knew that it was just about the ideal place ; what was more, one of its banks had worn away, bringing to light the side of another sunken wall, perfect for working out from. With singing heart, he pushed the felt out of sight beneath the hawthorns ; then absent-mindedly fingering the lid and briar-pipe in his pocket, he turned for home.

Just wait till he told Roy about this !

3

The Art Competition

'Honest, Miss—I never even saw it!'

Brooksbank's voice was a convincing mixture of protest and alarm, making Miss Seymour turn her inquiring gaze on to the other boy standing before her.

'He's telling lies,' asserted Colin vigorously. 'He couldn't *help* seeing it; I put it down right beside me!'

'You're sure you didn't kick it under a bush by accident, Colin?' asked the teacher, controlling her impatience. From the corner of her eye she could see that the front rows were listening attentively; she'd give another three minutes to 'Trant versus Brooksbank' and that would have to be all.

'But there weren't any bushes, Miss,' Colin was saying, 'just plain grass. He *must* have taken it—else it'd still be there!'

'That'll do, Colin,' said Miss Seymour sharply. She turned back to the ginger-haired boy. She would not put him above taking someone else's pencil-case, but on the other hand Colin Trant had only been in her class a week; he seemed truthful but it was rather early to know for certain. What a fine send-off for Monday morning!

'Did you see where he put this pencil-case, when you met him on Saturday, Victor?' she demanded.

'No, Miss,' said Brooksbank, looking her boldly in the face. 'I never even noticed he had one! He—he's making it all up—just because I pulled his leg about where he comes from.'

At the back of the class, Mary Deason and Roger Green were having a tug-of-war over the same library book. Miss Seymour sighed; thank heaven for those polythene covers.

'You ought to know better than to tease a new boy, Victor,' she said reprovingly. 'Sit down.' She had deliberately raised her voice, and the book-battle ceased discreetly.

As Brooksbank triumphantly ambled back to his seat at the back, Miss Seymour got up from behind her desk.

'I'm afraid it doesn't look as if he's got it, Colin,' she said kindly, 'though I'm sorry you've lost something you're so fond of. It might have slid down the bank and got buried in the grass somewhere—I'd have another look tonight.'

Colin resumed his seat, burning with resentment. It wasn't fair. Brooksbank had lied straight to her face, and had got away with it. He took out his spelling book and forced himself to begin the date; his hand was trembling.

The first lessons were no more than a background murmur to his angry thoughts. After playtime he managed to get his feelings more under control, but even his favourite lesson—the Class Project about Wheatleigh's industries—raised only a lukewarm interest that morning.

It was Miss Seymour's question just before twelve o'clock that made him prick up his ears.

'Which of you would like to enter a Painting Competition?'

Was it imagination, or did her eyes rest on him for a second?

About a dozen girls and boys raised their hands cautiously, but Colin's remained steadfastly on the desk. Drawing, yes—he'd have entered like a shot; but he wasn't going to make a fool of himself, pretending he could paint.

'Good. Hands down.' She took a newspaper-cutting from her desk. 'As some of you know, our local paper holds an Art Competition every spring. Well, in last Friday's *Wheatleigh Mail* they announced all the rules. The subject this year is "My Ideal Holiday"; and the closing date is 31st May. So you've over thirteen weeks to do it.'

She pinned up the paper on the notice-board by the door and was about to return to her desk, when a hand went up at the rear of the room.

'Yes, Victor?'

'Please, Miss, what are the prizes?'

Smiles flickered round the classroom. Trust Brooksbank to think of that!

'The first prize is two pounds, the second one pound, and the third ten shillings,' replied Miss Seymour tersely. 'But I hope no one here will enter just for the sake of the money ; it's meant for those who like painting for its own sake . . . Now then : hands up once more, those who are thinking of entering.'

This time Colin refused to meet her gaze. With prizes like that, there'd be certain to be far better painters than him. He kept his hand down.

But he could not resist stopping behind when the class was dismissed. There wouldn't be any harm in reading what the newspaper had said. Several others crowded with him round the notice-board, but not Brooksbank, of course ; Colin could hear him announcing in the cloakroom that he knew much better ways of wasting his time.

Like pinching pencil-cases, thought Colin ironically.

He concentrated on the newspaper cutting.

THE WHEATLEIGH MAIL
JUNIOR ART COMPETITION

Entries are invited for the next competition. The subject chosen is ' My Ideal Holiday '. It is hoped that each boy and girl will illustrate the kind of holiday he or she would like best.

It could be a seaside holiday on a sunny, crowded beach, or hiking in lonely parts of the Welsh mountains ; it might be canoeing on the river, or high-diving at an open-air swimming-pool. It could be a spot of quiet fishing in the lake, or an exhausting cycle-race ; a stay at a bustling holiday camp, a visit to a fairground,

or just a peaceful away-from-it-all rest at a country
village.

Remember the rules :—

1. All entrants must be under 16 years of age.
2. Do not make your painting larger than 15 inches
   by 12.
3. The prizes will be two pounds, one pound, and
   ten shillings.
4. The Judges' decision will be final.

You have plenty of time : the closing date is 31st
May. But start thinking now—what is the Ideal
Holiday for you ? Let us see your answer in our
Spring Painting Competition.

With a start, Colin suddenly found he was the only
one left at the notice-board, and that from behind her
desk Miss Seymour was eyeing him curiously. With
an elaborate grimace of indifference towards all Painting
Competitions, he scuttled for the cloakroom.

But the newspaper had given an exciting drift to his
thoughts ; and it was a strangely hopeful Colin who
wandered homeward.

' Well, rather you than me, going out on a night
like this,' declared Mrs Trant. ' When I got that coal
in, it was fair freezing.'

Colin considered asking impishly what frozen coal
looked like ; then he remembered that it was Monday
and that his mother's temper was uncertain on baking
days.

' I'm only going to meet Roy, Mum,' he said perkily, his hand already on the back-door latch.

' Well, mind you don't come in the wrong side of nine o'clock again,' warned his mother, as she put the last of her warm scones into the larder. ' And just look at you ! Come here for a minute, and let me tuck your scarf in properly. If I didn't watch you, you'd wander round looking like that scarecrow in Baxter's orchard.' Her hot, plump hands straightened the scarf. ' You remember that scarecrow ? ' she added softly.

' Course I remember it,' grunted Colin ; he must have drawn it a dozen times.

' Still wish you were back, love ? ' She was pulling his collar up, and her eyes were suddenly kind.

Taken by surprise, Colin nodded. He remembered the open fields, the exhilarating wind on the hill-tops ; they made Wheatleigh seem some sort of drab pit, with its cliff-like factories and houses leaning over you wherever you looked. Then he saw the troubled frown forming in his mother's eyes and added swiftly, ' But I'll soon get used to things here, Mum.'

' That's the way, love.' Mrs Trant smiled fondly, then added : ' There are some things I miss too—but, well, your dad gets better money on the railway . . .'

She gave a last affectionate tug at his lapel and then hustled to the oven for the fruit cake. Colin paused, his hand half-way to the latch once more. The words of the newspaper came simmering up again in his mind ; and now seemed a good time to ask.

' Mum.'

'What is it, love?' Mrs Trant blinked as the hot air billowed out from the oven, and then began to grope inside with hands immersed in her thick, protective towel.

'If we've got more money coming in, does—does that mean we'll be having a holiday this year?'

Her face apple-pink from the heat, his mother straightened up and grabbed a kitchen knife.

'It does,' she replied shortly, driving the blade cautiously into the cake to test it.

Colin swallowed excitedly. They had not gone away for a proper holiday for several years—indeed, for as far back as he could remember. It hadn't seemed to matter much at Cullerton : there had always been the common, the woods and the brook—and the farms had always wanted boys, especially at harvest-time. But here in the drab maze of Wheatleigh, a holiday suddenly seemed very important.

'Where're we going to, Mum?' he asked fervently.

Dubiously Mrs Trant eyed the knife-blade. 'Ilfracombe,' she said.

'What's it like?'

'Oh—beaches, and rocky cliffs and nice parks.'

Hesitantly she straightened up.

'When—when are we going?' asked Colin breathlessly.

'Oh, ages yet : last week in August . . .'

Swallowing hard, Colin slipped hastily out into the frosty evening.

He trotted through the lamp-lit streets, partly to

make up for lost time and partly to keep out the cold. He was exultant with relief. He felt as if he had been gradually sucked into a whirlpool—and then all at once a life-line had been thrown to him. The maelstrom of roaring traffic, of bustling people, of narrow streets and sky-blotting factories, still held him—but he knew he would not drown, he knew there was a way of escape not far off.

He wondered how he would have felt if his mother had said no, they still couldn't afford a holiday this year. The thought made his throat feel thick and choked. To be pinned inside Wheatleigh, like a dead butterfly pinned up in a museum ; to be starved for two years or more of the vast, open countryside . . . With an effort, he wiped the idea from his mind ; he supposed there were poor families like that, but luckily his was not one of them.

When at last he reached the wasteland and made his way across to the hawthorn clump, it was to find Roy already hard at work hammering some struts into the cracks in the half-buried wall. They had agreed that this would be the best way of preventing the roofing-felt from sagging in the middle.

Tugging the roll from its hiding-place, he sent it bouncing down into the hollow. It thumped against the iron sheet they had collected for a door, making his friend jump. He spun round, nearly dropping his old hammer.

' Oh, it's you ! ' he panted wryly. ' I'd given you up for dead ! '

He turned again to his battering, and with a grin Colin went down to help.

Roy Smithson was a tall, dark-haired boy whom Colin had met at school. He was in a higher class for he was over a year older, and at first Colin had thought this would soon break their friendship. As that first week had passed, however, they had talked and played in the school yard more and more freely ; they had gone on to swapping stamps and comics, with a quick understanding of each other's likes and dislikes ; and by the end of the week they had begun to play together in the streets after four o'clock.

Yet there was something unusual about Roy ; at times he would become gruff and bad-tempered, and behave as if he were torn with some strange resentment. He seemed as lonely in his class at school as Colin was in Miss Seymour's ; and the younger boy sensed that it was probably this feeling of loneliness which had drawn them together. But what it was that often made Roy hard to get along with, Colin had so far been unable to discover.

What had cemented their friendship above all else, however, had been Colin's discovery of the Old Field (as they had immediately named it). They had determinedly spent most of Sunday rummaging round all the scrap-heaps Roy knew ; then they had begun working the results into the shape of a hut. Here Colin had come into his own—he had built scores of dens in Cullerton woods ; and as the hut took shape Roy had to admit he learned a great deal.

There was nothing rickety, nothing wasted. Stout corner-poles were driven firmly into the ground; between them was raised a painstaking jigsaw of timber, matchboard and corrugated iron. Everything was bound ingeniously into place with stout wire, and fitted snugly up to the stone wall which was going to take the main weight of the roof.

With Roy holding the sticks in place and Colin driving them in, they made short work of what was left.

'See any sign of our good friend as you came across?' panted Roy at last.

Colin paused. 'Which friend?'

'Old Carrot-Hair.'

'Oh, him . . . No.' Colin banged the last strut further into its crack and went on to describe what had happened with Miss Seymour that morning.

'Your pencil-case's gone for good, then,' declared Roy. 'He'll tell his mother he swapped something for it, and keep it at home from now on.'

Colin gave one final, bitter blow on the stick before him. He too knew he would never see it again. Gulping down his feelings, he went to help Roy unroll the felt.

They found there was enough for a double thickness on top, as well as a good overlap all round. Hoisting it across the struts, they positioned it so that its edges were protruding over the top of the hut's walls. Then Colin astutely produced a tobacco-tin of one-inch nails; and taking care that its rear edge remained snuggled up to the stone wall, the two boys began to tack the felt into place.

' We can furnish it with orange-boxes or something,' panted Colin, banging away vigorously with half a brick ; Roy had the hammer.

The elder boy nodded. ' I know where we can get some old lino,' he offered. ' The rag-and-bone chap'll let me have a bit, 'cos I often help him in the holidays.'

For a moment, Colin was puzzled, not quite sure what a rag-and-bone man was ; then Roy's words brought back something more important to his mind.

' Talking of holidays—you know what ? ' he blurted. ' I've found out we're going to Ilfracombe for ours ! '

Roy tugged at the stiff canvas. ' So what ? ' he grunted.

Colin recognized the sudden sourness in his voice, but felt too excited to care.

' It'll be our first real one for years ! ' he went on. ' You see, at Cullerton, Dad didn't earn much, and after Tim was born, Mum couldn't manage at all, so we moved here. Now we're a bit better off ; so we're having our first seaside holiday ! '

He battered in another nail so gleefully that the whole hut shook.

Roy shrugged, and bent down to the tobacco-tin. ' That's fine,' he said dryly.

Colin realized his resentment, and tried to turn it.

' What about your holidays ? ' he asked.

' Well, what about 'em ? '

' I mean, where're you going ? '

'I've told you,' said Roy; he drew the felt tight and hammered a nail in viciously. 'I'll probably be helping the rag-and-bone chap,' he grinned; but there was no amusement in his eyes.

'But your mum and dad'll be taking you to the seaside or somewhere, won't they?' blurted Colin in surprise.

Roy paused, his hammer in mid air. He stared strangely, almost fiercely, at Colin.

Then all at once something inside him seemed to give.

'Look: I haven't got a father,' he said; his voice was loud and harsh. 'He died last year . . . My mum's got me and my two baby sisters to look after : she has to work at the factory part-time, to earn enough—and she does wonders on what bit of money she gets . . . But there's not enough for any jaunts to Ilfracombe or anywhere else, understand ?'

His eyes blazed challengingly.

Colin swallowed and nodded ; the edge of the roofing-felt burst free from his numbed fingers.

He lowered his eyes. Automatically he pressed the fold back into place and nailed it down. Now he understood many things.

All at once the thought of Ilfracombe did not seem quite so exciting : for Roy would be staying behind—pinned inside Wheatleigh.

It was a very thoughtful Colin who arrived home later that evening.

4

The Labourers' Revolt

The month of March passed as briskly as its bold winds, that tossed the new tree-buds in the park and swept dry each day's gleaming pavements. And with April's milder weather and lighter evenings, Mr Trant, after a few prods from his wife, began his share of the spring-cleaning at last.

It took him two weeks to dig the long, deep trenches that would take the conservatory's walls. They cost Mr Trant much backache from pick and shovel work ; in fact, rather more than he had bargained for, because instead of Colin appearing eagerly each evening, and having to be hauled out of the sticky earth and set to work removing it, Colin had surprisingly shown no interest whatever.

Using the bricks from the old greenhouse, Mr Trant methodically laid the foundations in each trench on Saturday evening ; as he worked, he found himself pondering about Colin harder than ever. There was something on the boy's mind, for sure.

Mr Trant completed another course of bricks, then turned with aching back to plant his trowel in the glistening mound of cement. Well, talk of the devil : out of the corner of his eye he saw that Colin was leaning against the door-jamb, eyeing him intently.

'Dad.'

Mr Trant wiped a grey hand on the thigh of his boiler-suit, and glanced round. 'Well, son?'

'If you wanted to get a lot of money, Dad, how'd you set about it?'

Mr Trant sat on his heels.

'If I wanted a lot of money?' he repeated with a grin. 'What makes you think I don't?'

'Seriously, Dad,' protested Colin.

His father stood up, and thoughtfully tried to rub the small of his back.

'When I was your age,' he grunted, 'there was no end to the jobs we did to raise money for our footballs or cricket bats . . . We collected old lemonade bottles and got a few coppers on them from the village shop; we hiked to outlying farms with their evening papers; and Heaven knows how many gardens we weeded and hedges we clipped. Any of those any good?'

Colin shook his head, knowing that if he hiked and weeded and clipped till Doomsday, it wouldn't bring him a fraction of what the Smithsons needed. Diffidently he crouched beside the cement hummock and began to work the trowel up and down, making a satisfying, ridged pattern.

'Suppose you wanted to buy a—a—a huge house, Dad,' he persisted. 'How would you get the money?'

This time his father stared at him in earnest.

'Well—I could scratch my head a bit more over the Pools,' he began with a self-conscious grin; then, noticing Colin's irritation, he added more kindly, ' But if I was really desperate, I'd try to borrow the money.'

His son looked up hopefully.

' Who from ? ' he asked ; the trowel was poised motionless in his hand.

' A building society,' replied Mr Trant, managing to keep the amusement out of his voice.

' Do they lend *anybody* money ? '

' Good Lord, no ! ' chuckled his father. ' Only to people they know can pay them back—plus a good profit, of course. I borrowed the money for *this* house from a building society, but they waited till I'd landed that railway job first.'

There was silence. Colin looked down listlessly. His pattern in the cement had oozed back into flatness.

' What's this all about, anyway, Colin ? ' asked his father suddenly. ' You thinking of changing your hut for a mansion, or something ? '

Colin shook his head. Wearily he wedged the trowel back into its hummock.

' Then why all this quiz about getting money ? ' said Mr Trant casually.

' Oh, nothing, Dad,' muttered Colin. He straightened up and added : ' Just something Miss Seymour asked us, that's all.'

Mr Trant grunted non-committally, recognizing the evasion for what it was.

' Sorry I couldn't help,' he remarked evenly.

' That's all right, Dad,' said Colin stolidly. ' Thanks just the same.'

Mr Trant bent thoughtfully over the new brickwork and began to make up for lost time : it would soon be too dark for any more. Funny that it was high finance the lad was worrying his head over.

Colin strolled moodily out of the yard and into the dusky street. Dolefully he fingered the metal lid in his pocket. So that was that ; anyway, the whole idea had been up in the clouds right from the start, he told himself.

Ever since Colin had begun Barnsley Road School, Wednesday afternoons in Class 3 were always ' Project ' time. The Project that term was Wheatleigh itself, for Miss Seymour believed her class should know as much as possible about the town most of them would grow up, work and live in. She also believed children learned more by ferreting out the facts for themselves, so that when they had been studying the town's geography, all the children had had to give a short talk on their fathers' work in the local industries. Even newcomer Colin had been roped in ; and with a lot of help from his father—plus a load of stage-fright from himself— he had managed to tell the class a few facts about Wheatleigh's railway system.

Since the middle of March, however, Miss Seymour had switched to the historical side : the whole class had visited the museum and seen the Stone Age axe-heads turned up by farmers' ploughs—also some Roman medallions and two great iron axes left by the Vikings after one of their raids.

On subsequent Wednesdays, Miss Seymour had passed rapidly through medieval times, and by the Wednesday following Mr Trant's first onslaught on his brick-laying, she had reached the early nineteenth century. At that time Wheatleigh was only a village of sixty cottages—'with its wheelwright always busy for the local farmers, and its blacksmith shoeing the mares of the gentry, while the grey-stone water-mill ground away steadily day after day at the corn of farmer and squire . . .'

Thus, that afternoon, Miss Seymour's voice described the Wheatleigh of long ago. And after the first ten minutes, Colin's mind unconsciously turned it down, in the way it could shut out the murmur of the television when he was drawing or reading.

Dully he remembered once more the fruitless talk with his father. That had been no help at all ; and a fortnight's holiday for four needed at least £50. He eyed his desk blankly : better stick to what he'd decided and stop moping. There were plenty of other things to worry about—for a start, whether he should after all enter that Art Competition . . .

' *Colin Trant !* '

Miss Seymour's voice rapped out sharply, tumbling him back into the world of classrooms and history projects.

' Y—yes, Miss ? '

' You haven't heard a word I said ! Victor Brooksbank, repeat the question for him.'

Colin heard the scrape of a chair at the back, followed

by the smirk in Brooksbank's voice : ' What was the work of a village squire about the year 1800, Miss.'

Colin stood up, his brain racing anxiously to recall what Miss Seymour had told them last week.

' The—the village squire lived in a big house, called —er—a manor house, Miss.'

' Go on.'

' And—and he was usually a rich farmer—and owned most of the land in the district, so nearly all the villagers worked for him, Miss. '

' Yes, go on.' At times she could be inexorable.

' Oh, I know ! He was boss over the farm-workers in other ways, too.' Colin's mind had miraculously cleared, bringing everything back. ' You see, he was generally the local magistrate as well ; and it was his job to decide what wages the farm-workers should get —and as he had to pay out the wages himself, he always decided on low ones ! '

' Good. You remembered it,' conceded Miss Seymour, her gaze softening a little. ' Now, sit down and don't fall asleep again. The rest of you, I'm going on from where Colin Trant left off.'

And as he sank gratefully into his seat, she went on to explain the three reasons why after 1815 the country squires became the most hated people in England.

First, it seemed they made vast profits by selling their corn at extortionate prices (taking advantage of a wheat shortage), while at the same time they paid their farm-workers less than ten shillings a week. Secondly, in order to make still more money, they took away the common land belonging to the villagers, and enclosed it into fields where they could sow more corn, with the result that the people could no longer grow their own vegetables or keep their own goats. And thirdly, the squires began to use threshing-machines ; these did the work that twenty men used to do before, so hundreds of labourers were thrown out of their jobs.

' These three things, low wages, the enclosing of their land, and the use of threshing-machines,' concluded Miss Seymour emphatically, ' made the country folk so desperately poor and hungry that by 1830 they could stand it no longer. They went to their local magistrates and demanded a basic wage of half a crown a day. And the magistrates, being farmers and wanting to keep their profits to themselves, refused to give any rise whatever. And then the trouble began.'

She paused, and gazed keenly at the class.

' What sort of trouble, Miss ? ' asked one of the girls, breaking the silence.

A hand shot up in the front row. ' I can guess, Miss.'

' All right, John. What sort of trouble ? '

' Please, Miss, they would all have banded together and marched up to the squire's manor house. And if he wouldn't give them more money then, they'd threaten to kill him and smash his house up ! '

' Yes,' said Miss Seymour, ' that's exactly what *did* happen in many parts of England. The farm-workers began to riot : they demanded money from the rich, they set fire to the farmers' hayricks and they wrecked all the threshing-machines they could get hold of. We call it the Last Labourers' Revolt. Their leader is supposed to have said : *We will destroy the corn stacks and the threshing-machines this year, next year we will have a turn with the parsons, and the third year we will make war upon the statesmen.* No wonder the country squires were terrified ! No wonder they called out the soldiers to protect them, or took their wives and valuables to a safer district ! And all this happened right here in Wheatleigh, as well.'

As her last words sank in, thirty pairs of eyes widened in sudden interest.

' Did—did they kill the squire here, Miss ? ' exclaimed someone.

Miss Seymour stepped back to her desk, and took up a thick, brown book.

' This is from the library,' she told them, opening it where an envelope had marked the page. ' It tells you a lot about what happened long ago in this town of ours, and when I've finished with it, some of you might like to get it out for yourselves. Now, I'm going to read to you what happened during the rioting in 1830.'

Colin leaned his elbows on his ink-stained desk lid, and watched her intently.

' *On the afternoon of September 6th, 1830, the squire —Charles Nathaniel Kemp—rejected for the third time in ten days the petition of the Wheatleigh farm-workers for a wage increase of one shilling a day. Discussing the labourers afterwards, he declared to the parson : " Ah, I should be well pleased if a plague were to break out among them, and then I should have their carcases as manure, and*

43

right good stuff it would make for my crops." Perhaps this speech was intended only as a brutal jest; but among the villagers, when they heard it, it produced not mirth but rage.

'That evening as the squire drove back to the manor house, a hungry mob was waiting at the lodge gates, uttering threats and throwing stones. There were bitter cries that Kemp, renowned for possessing the finest collection of silver in the county, was harsh enough to refuse the workers one shilling a day. For the following three days a desperate crowd gathered each evening outside his estate.

'In passing, it is interesting to note that what was then the site of these angry demonstrations is now one of the quietest spots in modern Wheatleigh, a forsaken wasteland between the new council-housing estate and the belt of factories built since the Second World War. This broad field overgrown with bramble and gorse still holds beneath its soil the worn bricks that were part of Kemp's fine manor house over a century ago.'

As Miss Seymour paused for breath, Colin stared, petrified. For an instant the room seemed to whirl around him. Then the teacher continued steadily:

'It was on the fourth evening that matters came to a head. It seems that the squire's gardener had lit a bonfire in the grounds to burn some rubbish. During the day there had come rumours of yet another rise in the price of bread, putting it quite out of reach of the poorest families; and by now it must have become clear to them that despite their threats, Kemp did not intend to grant their demand. Probably it entered their minds that more drastic methods of persuasion might succeed. Whatever it was that caused the overflowing of their temper, the result was terrible indeed.

'Using burning sticks seized from the bonfire, the bitter menfolk set fire to the squire's orchards and outhouses. Due to the dry summer, the fire spread rapidly, travelling from the orchard to the stables, and then creeping on to the manor house itself. The terrified servants came out running, and would have tried to form a bucket-chain to save the house, but the jubilant crowd drove them off.

'Kemp, knowing he would get no mercy from the starving villagers, remained in the burning house as long as he dared, and then made a dash for the stables, probably hoping to escape on horseback. In their grim rejoicing, the labourers nearly failed to notice him, and by the time they gave chase, he was half-way to his goal. Such a lead had he that it is likely he would have escaped easily, but for the intervention of Fate.

'The stable roof, which had been burning steadily, groaned and sagged as he entered; and no sooner had the villagers run another yard nearer, than it collapsed in a holocaust of red flame and black smoke. No one, friend or foe, was madman enough to enter the furnace after him, and Charles Kemp perished in the blaze.'

There were stifled gasps from some of the girls. Colin sat bolt-upright, his startled eyes never leaving Miss Seymour's face for an instant. At this point she hesitated, almost closing the book; then, seeing there

45

were six minutes left of the lesson, she decided to go on.

' *As not a finger was lifted to save it, the manor house and everything in it were completely burnt and levelled by the blaze. Several days elapsed before Kemp's friends and solicitor began looking through the ruins for articles worth salvaging. It is commonly believed they were especially seeking the squire's famous collection of silver, which was of great value. However, no trace of it was ever found, and it was assumed that either it had been stolen during the rioting by some of the villagers, or else Kemp had previously removed it to a Bank or the home of a friend—for many wealthy landlords took similar precautions during those troubled times.*

' *What was discovered, however, was an iron deed-box. When it was forced open, its contents—the squire's will, deeds of property, and several letters—were found to be scorched and crinkled, but not illegible. In due course the solicitor posted these to Kemp's relatives, who had emigrated some years previously.*

' *According to the solicitor's private records, from which our information is taken, he shortly received instructions that the manor-house ruins should be searched again most thoroughly. Kemp's daughter, writing from abroad, where she had perused the letters and documents sent her, gave a most precise description of her father's snuff-box, which, she stated, it was vitally important to find. James Whittan, the solicitor, assured her in his reply that the ruins had already been most thoroughly searched, and that everything of value had been forwarded to her immediately after. Catherine Kemp replied by return post, insisting that the snuff-box contained more than would be supposed, and that it must be found.*

' Whittan therefore faithfully organised a second combing of the manor's remains, in the course of which, following Catherine Kemp's explicit instructions, every brick was overturned and laid low. At the end of the third week, the snuff-box was discovered and sent immediately to Kemp's daughter—but not before James Whittan had himself examined it most carefully, and discovered nothing in it whatever. Apparently Catherine Kemp found the same, for in future correspondence with Whittan she never mentioned it again, although she enquired regularly until her death in 1871, whether her father's silver collection had ever been traced.

' Thus ended the sorry episode of the 1830 hunger riots in Wheatleigh.'

Miss Seymour raised her eyes from the page, and slowly closed the book. For a moment the room was silent. Colin sat motionless, his mind spinning with excitement.

Then there was a movement at the back of the class.

' Yes, Victor ? ' said Miss Seymour.

' Please, Miss, what's a silver collection ? ' asked Brooksbank innocently. ' Like the one we have in church on Sundays ? '

' No—and don't try to be funny,' replied the teacher sharply. ' Charles Kemp collected articles made of silver, just as some boys collect stamps or model trains. He gradually built up a huge collection of table-ware and ornaments—things like plates, dishes, vases, goblets and cutlery ; they were all made from the finest silver, and decorated with patterns and pictures engraved by the best silversmiths of his day. So you can imagine why it was worth a fortune ! '

She picked up the library book once more.

' This is the kind of thing he collected,' she announced, finding the page she wanted and holding it up for them to see. ' This is a drawing of his silver snuff-box. Notice the raised pattern on the sides—called filigree— and his initials engraved on the lid. By the way, this is the snuff-box his daughter was so eager to get hold of, and then changed her mind once she'd got it.'

Colin's heart gave a queer lurch. The illustration, done in the thin, spidery lines of bygone days, showed a small, square box, its sides decorated with clinging ivy leaves of silver. Its lid he had first seen over six weeks before : it was small enough to fit the top of his money-box, and it was lettered C.N.K.

5

The Silver Lid

There were very few things that easy-going Mr Trant insisted on. One of these, since their move into Wheatleigh, was that once a week his wife should have a break from housework. He wanted to keep a wife, not a charlady, he asserted with twinkling eyes in reply to Mrs Trant's first flustered arguments; and as soon as baby Tim was old enough to manage without a feed and change of nappy every few hours, he had begun their Wednesday evening ritual of going to the cinema.

Since Colin had to baby-sit, they visited the 'first house', in order to be back before his bedtime. This meant Mr Trant had to hurry home from the railway at half past five, and try to concertina his meal from its usual half-hour into ten minutes. With his wife worrying that he'd never do it in time and fussing that it would ruin his digestion, he nevertheless always finished with a couple of minutes to spare. Then it would be his turn to wait, while Mrs Trant dashed upstairs to have a last look at Tim and to put on her hat and coat. It was a weekly miracle how they managed to bustle out of the house before six.

With Tim tucked fast asleep in his cot upstairs, and the house all to himself, Colin used to enjoy those

Wednesday evenings. He liked the lonely cosiness of the living-room, strangely big and silent ; and there was the delicious half-bleak, half-proud feeling of responsibility. If the fire went out, if someone knocked, or if Tim woke up, he could rely on no one but himself.

Those three hours of freedom brought other things too ; he could let his model railway sprawl over the entire floor, winding in and out of the table legs ; he could unearth his Meccano set from the cupboard, and build a gantry-crane or hover-craft ; or he could switch off the light and make entrancing, gloomy caverns among the chairs and stool and sofa—with a little imagination you became Stone Age Man, and the orange-snaked fire in the grate your only protection from mammoths and sabre-toothed tigers . . .

That Wednesday, however, things were different.

For a long time after Mr Trant had hastily slammed the front door, Colin stared blankly into the fire, undecided as to what to do. Of course, there was always the television set, squatting in the corner like a patient genie ; but it was a relief to be free from its glare for a while.

None of the usual games appealed to him either. Even the thought of sketching made him feel strangely disgruntled. How about a book, then ?

He wandered over to his father's bookshelf. Two-thirds of it were devoted to ' Do-it-yourself ' and carpentry manuals, but there was an old core of more serious books which Mr Trant had lovingly collected over many years. Colin drew out the heavy volume he had been meaning to read for several months, all about how to understand famous paintings.

The Smithsons . . .

Colin had never found it as difficult to concentrate on anything as that book ; he had to read the first page three times. It was only after getting as far as the fifth that he realized he was wasting his time. It was like trying to draw with the wrong end of your pencil.

With a sigh, he gave in. Closing the book, he sprawled on his back on the hearth-rug, and stared disconsolately at the ceiling.

The Smithsons . . .

He suddenly realized how fiercely his heart was pounding. A mile away in the grey April night lay the Old Field, waiting—waiting for him and Roy. Something inside him seemed tensed up, ready to burst.

He grimaced at the rash drift of his thoughts, and tightened his lips. He must force himself to keep calm —get through the evening somehow or other. To-morrow wouldn't be so bad, there'd be school to take his mind off it ; Thursdays meant extra arithmetic in the morning, and handwork in the afternoon.

With great determination he opened the book once more : that way Thursday evening would come more quickly.

Next day, after school was over at last, Colin took Roy straight to the Old Field. Slipping unobserved through the fence, as usual they looked round cautiously from the top of the nearby hillock. But of Brooksbank, or of anyone else, there was no sign. Unbelievably quiet and deserted, the wasteland stretched away below them as though nothing eventful had happened there for centuries.

' I came across it just here,' said Colin, ' when I was looking for my pencil-case.'

Roy looked down at the grassy bank and sniffed.

' Still think it was the same lid, then ? ' he remarked cynically.

' I've told you, Miss Seymour showed us a picture ! ' retorted Colin.

' Must be loads of small, square lids round here,' grunted the older boy. ' Think of all the stuff we've seen : cocoa-tins, baccy-tins, petrol-cans . . . Could've been any of those—or even something off a bike ! '

' What—with the exact letters on the top ? ' replied Colin sarcastically. ' Come on—race you to the hut ! '

And as he tore past the brambles and ditches, with one strangely calm part of his mind he observed the spring-green tips on the boughs and the pennons of new grass underfoot : in a few weeks everything would look completely different from when he'd first sketched it in February.

Roy's long legs made him an easy winner. He slid the corrugated iron back from the doorway, and was comfortably settled on an apple-box by the time Colin panted his way in.

' Now then,' declared Roy, in a much more amiable mood, ' having put you in your place, we'll get down

52

to business ! Let's suppose it *is* the same lid : so what ? '

Sinking down on to an empty oil-drum, Colin
gathered his breath ; and then mustering all his patience,
he began.

First he went over everything again : how in 1830
the Old Field had been the squire's estate, and how
Nathaniel Kemp had been killed in the fire started by
the desperate labourers ; how his valuable collection
of silver had never been found in the ruins, and was
thought to have been stolen ; and how eager his
daughter had been to find the snuff-box.

' According to the solicitor—Whittan, or something
—he found it and sent it to her, knowing that whatever
old Kemp's documents had told her, there was nothing
valuable in it at all,' concluded Colin. ' And once she'd
seen it for herself, she must've agreed, for she never
mentioned it again, though for the rest of her life she
kept on asking him if the silver had turned up.'

Roy gazed out at the nearby factory wall ; a glimmer
of understanding appeared in his dark eyes.

' You think the squire hid the silver 'cos he knew
there'd be trouble ? ' he said slowly. ' And he left some
sort of clue in his snuff-box, in case something happened
to him ? '

Colin nodded. ' Miss Seymour said loads of rich
people took their valuables to a Bank or hid them at
a friend's house,' he went on, eagerly. ' Kemp must
have done the same—and those documents Whittan sent
to the daughter must have told her there was a clue in
his snuff-box saying where he'd hidden the silver ! '

' You mean, like someone's address ? ' ventured Roy.
' Or a map.'

There was a short silence. Roy got up and stood pensively in the doorway.

' If you're right,' he grunted suddenly, ' why didn't they manage to find his clue once they'd got the snuff-box ? '

' Because they *didn't* find the snuff-box—at least, not the whole of it ! ' exclaimed Colin triumphantly. ' When the house was burnt down, the lid somehow got broken off; Whittan found only the box half. And when Catherine Kemp got it, and found it was broken and empty, she must've thought——' He stopped and grinned. ' Well—what would *you* have thought ? '

Roy frowned; his fingers picked absently at an overhanging edge of roofing-felt. ' Dunno——' he muttered.

Then all at once his eyes brightened. ' I—I suppose I'd have thought the clue must have fallen out ages ago; and—and that the map—or whatever it was—had got burnt in the fire ! '

' Of course ! ' grinned Colin. ' You wouldn't have bothered about not finding the lid, would you ? '

' Suppose not,' admitted Roy; then he added perplexedly, ' but what's the point, then ? '

Colin eyed him shrewdly. ' How do we know Kemp didn't put his clue in the snuff-box *lid* instead of in the box ? '

Roy stared.

And then, unable to contain himself any longer, Colin drew his hand from his pocket and held it out. In his palm lay the small, square lid, now cleaned of all its dried clay, and with the letters C.N.K. gleaming black upon it.

'Read what's inside,' he ordered tersely.

His heart hammering like a train-piston, Roy took it and turned it over.

At first he could make nothing out; then, screwing up his eyes a little, he noticed some faint marks—tiny letters cut into the silver!

They were engraved in a decorative, flowing script —both leisurely and graceful like the tendrils of the ivy on the church wall ; and they were arranged in four neat lines.

> *Marry the steeple*
> *To yonder grindstone.*
> *With threaded needle*
> *Is silver sown.*

6

The Tight-rope

During that week Mr Trant had used the lighter evenings to complete his damp-course and raise the conservatory wall to two feet six inches. Above that he intended to put panes of glass which would reach up to a sloping roof over the back door. Originally, the following weekend was the time he'd intended starting the woodwork—he had already collected the timber for the sills and window-frames—but after Saturday breakfast he suddenly discovered that six-inch nails somehow weren't among the odds and ends always finding their way into his overalls. Accordingly Colin was given orders to buy some from Boulton's.

The two boys met as usual at the corner of Sutcliff Street. To Colin's relief, the older boy did not seem to mind this compulsory change of plan. This was because going to Boulton's gave Roy the chance to visit the river, which, although it flowed past the bottom of Bravender Place, his street, was tantalizingly sealed off by a row of green spiked railings and a sheer drop beyond.

Boulton's was a builders' merchant's—two or three warehouses round an enormous yard cluttered with mounds of sand and girders and bricks. Its chief merit in Roy's eyes was the fact that as it lay close to the river Thorpe about half a mile beyond the High Street, he could come back by the short cut along the river bank with little chance of being spotted by anyone who might inform his mother ; for since a small girl had once been drowned at the spot nicknamed ' the Tight-rope ', Mrs Smithson had put it strictly out of bounds.

That morning the water looked so sluggish and quiet when he and Colin eventually reached it that it was quite easy to convince himself that the rule could be forgotten ; while to his companion, the grey slithering ripples beside them spoke of something quite different : the glorious times when he'd caught minnows and sticklebacks in Cullerton brook.

' Any more Sherlock Holmes stuff today?'

Colin returned abruptly to the present time. He looked at Roy in bewilderment for a moment ; then the ironic grin on his friend's face told him they were back to the old argument again.

' There might be,' he replied enigmatically. He fingered the parcel of nails in his pocket, and for a minute the two boys wandered in silence along the muddy path. Deep inside him, Colin chuckled : it was like two boxers cagily sizing each other up.

They reached the place where the brick wall beside them jutted out greedily, leaving only a five-foot grass verge ; Roy made the first exploratory jab.

' If you ask me, old Kemp must have been nuts.'

Colin grinned. ' Why ? ' he asked innocently.

' That poem : *Marry the steeple !* ' growled Roy

scornfully. 'How the dickens do you think you can do that ?'

'You could if you were another steeple, I suppose,' said Colin cheerfully.

His companion snorted, and fiercely pushed his black fringe out of his eyes. With a grin Colin felt for something in his right-hand trouser pocket.

'Read that,' he commanded, handing over a neatly folded bit of notepaper.

Roy opened it disgruntledly. In Colin's tidy hand-writing was written : 'Dictionary definition of *Marry* : to join in wedlock, or (archaic) to unite very closely.'

He read it twice, then looked up blankly.

'Well, what's the point of that ?' he remarked.

'Elementary, my dear Watson !' teased Colin in return. The river was beginning to curve a little to the right, and the High Street bridge was creeping into view half a mile ahead.

'What's this word in brackets—Secret Service code ?' Roy demanded dryly. 'It says *ar-chick* or something.'

'It's pronounced *ar-kay-ic*,' corrected Colin. 'It means "old-fashioned".'

'Like it comes from the Ark, I suppose ?' grunted Roy.

'Might do,' said Colin vaguely ; he had never thought of it like that before. 'Anyway, *that* meaning of *marry* fits the verse better, doesn't it ?'

'How ?' asked Roy grimly.

Colin took back the paper, and produced in its stead the snuff-box lid. Glancing inside, he read out :

> *' Unite the steeple*
> *To yonder grindstone '*

' Sure ! That makes much better sense,' commented Roy sarcastically. ' People are uniting steeples to grindstones every day ! '

Colin flushed, and slipped the lid back into his pocket.

' It means some *special* way of joining them,' he remarked doggedly. ' A way we haven't worked out yet.'

With a muddy shoe, Roy scuffed a stone into the ripples of the river. ' Maybe,' he grunted ; then added sourly, ' First, find your grindstone.'

And that was the real trouble, thought Colin ; he could think of only two things a grindstone was used for—sharpening knives and grinding corn. And when they'd done Wheatleigh's industries in their Class Project, they hadn't come across either of them. In fact, the only grindstone he'd ever seen had been in a photograph in a travel book.

With a sigh, he followed Roy warily round a broad patch of mud ; another five minutes and they'd be clambering up the stone steps on to the bridge, and picking their way home up the crowded High Street.

Or would they ? Immediately in front of them a tall, grey-stone building jutted out through the brick wall, and seemed to swallow up completely the grass bank they were walking along. And as they drew near, Colin saw that its large, rough-hewn blocks rose straight up out of the leaden surface of the water.

'What now?' he muttered in puzzlement, as they halted where the grass verge sloped down to meet the see-sawing water.

'Recognize it?' countered Roy, jerking his dark head of hair at the building.

It was massive, whichever way you looked at it : its outer wall breasted the water for thirty or forty yards before it allowed the river bank to reappear and meander on towards the bridge ; furthermore it seemed to reach back from the water's edge equally as far,

though Colin couldn't see it all the way because of the side-wall they had been following ; while as for its height—the building soared upwards for at least three times as high as an ordinary house, and ended in an enormous peak of a roof.

And then Colin knew it. He had drawn it at least twice from the Old Field ; after the steeple, it was the tallest building you could see. Miss Seymour had once mentioned that it was a printer's and stationer's ; now what was its name ?

' My uncle works there,' remarked Roy proudly.

' Remington's ? ' blurted Colin suddenly.

' Near enough : Rimmington's,' declared Roy. ' My Uncle Phil drives their van.'

Colin turned back the way they had come.

' Come on,' he grunted, ' or we'll never get back before dinner. Did you forget you couldn't get through to the bridge this way or something ? '

Roy stayed where he was.

' What's wrong with the Tight-rope ? ' he said.

Colin turned round and followed the direction of Roy's eyes.

At first sight, the jutting wall had appeared to soar out of the water quite sheer ; Colin now noticed that this was not so : about two feet above the surface the wall was cut back six inches. It left a ledge no wider than a handspan, connecting their stretch of bank with the continuation over thirty yards away.

Colin glanced sharply at Roy's face : he didn't *seem* to be joking.

'Come on—I've done it before,' urged the older boy. '*I'm* not trailing right back to Boulton's.'

Colin nodded slowly. 'Let's see how you do it,' he said, speaking more boldly than he felt. If it came to 'dares', he'd hold his own with any townie.

Roy made it seem easy. With arms spread-eagled and chest hugging the wall, he edged his way across, stepping not more than a few inches at a time, yet moving rhythmically and surely. Even so, to Colin, who judged the river to be quite deep close to the building, it seemed long enough before his friend was grinning back at him from the further part of the bank.

'Your turn now!' called Roy.

Cautiously Colin put his left foot on to the ledge, and slid his left hand along the uneven, gritty stone wall. Then he took his right foot off the comforting grass and rested it lightly beside the other.

For an instant he paused, his heart hammering, perfectly poised on that meagre foothold. His cheek was pressed against the cold blocks, his eyes staring down at the thin ribbon he had to tread. He tried not to think of the glistening ripples he could just see out of the corner of his eye.

He began.

Moving one foot at a time, flattening himself desperately to the wall, he inched along. As long as you press against the wall, he told himself earnestly, you can't fall, it's just impossible.

Just impossible . . . And yet in no time at all his ankles were aching from the awkward position, and his feet were tired and clumsy with their shuffling steps. Raising his eyes for a second to where Roy was dabbling his fingers in the water, he wondered if he had reached half-way yet. It was a much longer distance than he had expected.

Quivering, his fingers worked themselves forward like spiders' legs on the stonework. The cement between the blocks had been worn back by age and weather, offering slight handholds every so far.

As he edged along, tense and perspiring, the cold-blooded part of his mind began to puzzle over the strangeness of the wall he was clinging to—better that than wondering about the current below him. Anyway it *was* strange that this was the only riverside building they'd met that ran straight down into the water—strange too that it had no windows ; it made him think of a blind man standing on the very edge of the pavement.

He paused a moment, letting his weary arms sag. The rough, black stones against his cheek, and the cracks between them, reminded him of something— the sunken wall on the Old Field. Perhaps they were equally as old ; perhaps this building had been standing when Kemp's manor house went up in flames. Come to think of it, there were probably lots of buildings in Wheatleigh that ancient. For one thing, the verse had mentioned a steeple.

All at once he realized what their next step should be. It was so obvious, the idea shot through him like an electric shock. For a second his startled fingers missed their grip. He felt himself swaying helplessly away from the wall.

Then his scrambling fingers found a hold, and he checked himself; another instant and he'd have—! Feeling slightly sick, he leaned again on the grimy stones, and waited till his heart had calmed a little.

'You taking all day?'

He looked up shakily. Roy was frowning at him impatiently.

I *must* be more than half-way by now, thought Colin feverishly; he seems much nearer than before.

'Keep your hair on,' he replied, trying to sound casual.

Using all the handholds he could find, he set off once more. Shuffle the left foot forward a few inches; bring the right one up. Grope along for another crack. Then the left foot again; then the right . . .

Two minutes later he stepped stiffly on to the grass next to Roy.

'S—sorry I took so long,' he muttered.

He felt for the package in his pocket, and thankfully set off towards the nearby bridge, eager to leave Rimmington's behind him. The only good thing about that place, he realized grimly, was that it had given him that sudden brainwave.

'That's all right,' grunted Roy magnanimously, falling into step beside him. 'It puts you one up on Brooksbank, anyway; last time I dared *him* to do the Tight-rope, he ran a mile.'

7

A Sermon on Weather-vanes

Monday was always Miss Seymour's hardest day, leaving her with big sets of English and History work to mark. After dismissing Class 3, it was her habit to settle determinedly at her desk and try to wade through the marking. However, there were always two or three lingerers who pestered her for jobs, or wanted to relate some out-of-school adventure; and she either accommodated them patiently or, when her energy and temper had worn a little thin, sent them all packing.

That particular Monday she was uncertain of her mood; the class had been extra restless during Music in the last period, and it had been an effort to hold down an answering irritability. She eyed the boy waiting meekly beside her desk, and decided she might as well hear him out. After all, she realized with slight surprise, he wasn't one of her regular time-wasters.

'Well, Colin, what is it?' she asked.

'About what you were saying the other day, Miss——' he began stolidly, having rehearsed himself carefully over the weekend.

'Oh yes,' she interrupted him with a bright smile. 'You've decided what you're going to paint for the Art Competition at last.'

Colin started; he'd completely forgotten about the *Wheatleigh Mail*.

'What's it going to be, then, Colin?' went on the teacher kindly. Though he had been in her class ever since February, she still couldn't help regarding him as a shy newcomer, who needed cautious encouragement.

Colin's mind had gone an uncomfortable blank. He had toyed with half a dozen ideas at first; and now that he needed them, not one would come back.

Miss Seymour came to his rescue.

'You want some suggestions?' she asked shrewdly. 'Well, if I were you, I'd choose something with no people in; there'll be children entering who'll be better than you at figure drawing, so I shouldn't try to compete with them. No, Colin—you do the thing you do best.' She nodded at one of the paintings pinned to the wall. 'That one you did of Cullerton woods—scarecrow and all—is the best landscape anyone's done for me yet. Why not do another for the competition?'

Colin hesitated, eyeing his painting thoughtfully. He could see now what was wrong with it; the colours were much too gaudy, making it look like a fairy glen from a picture book.

'Will you, Colin?'

He collected his wits and nodded. What he needed was a country scene nearby—a place he could keep looking at, to get the colours exactly right.

'Yes, Miss,' he agreed suddenly. 'I—I'll paint a landscape.'

'Good. Don't forget the last date for entering, will

you ? ' concluded Miss Seymour, turning back to the pile of exercise-books before her. ' The last day in May —so you've just about five weeks.'

' Yes, Miss,' murmured Colin awkwardly.

Miss Seymour took up her pencil, automatically drew the top book from the heap, and then realized Colin had not moved. He saw a tiny crease of impatience appear suddenly between her eyebrows.

' Something else, Colin ? ' she sighed.

' Yes, Miss,' he said, licking his lips. ' I—I've been thinking about what you told us in our Project lessons —all about Wheatleigh in the olden days.'

' In prehistoric times, you mean ? ' she asked, knowing what had impressed Class 3 the most. ' When the Ice Age glacier gouged out our valley ? '

' No, Miss. Not so long ago as that : when the squire's manor house was burnt down by the farm-workers in—in 1830 . . . I've been wondering, Miss, whether they had the same sort of things we have nowadays.'

' What sort of things, Colin ? ' asked Miss Seymour over-casually. Surely to goodness, Colin Trant wasn't going to ask that infuriating question about sputniks and television ? She credited him with more intelligence than that.

' Well, like—like our school, Miss—or that bridge over the river,' said Colin cautiously, for he thought it best to put in some ' red herrings ' first.

' Yes, there was a village school—not that the farm-labourers could afford to send their children to it, for it cost money ; but the better-off tradesmen like the blacksmith or the miller could manage it, I suppose . . . And there *was* an old packhorse bridge over the Thorpe in those days too—so you guessed right, didn't you ? ' she ended with a smile. ' Anything else ? ' she added, mechanically turning the pages of the waiting exercise-book.

' Did—did Wheatleigh have a church in Kemp's time, Miss ? The one across the river looks pretty old, the—the one with the steeple : did they use that one, do you think, Miss ? ' He flushed, for he hadn't meant to mention the steeple itself. He felt his throat tighten anxiously ; this was the question that had suddenly come to him that Saturday morning at Rimmington's.

' Well, there was bound to be some sort of church, Colin,' replied the teacher with a thoughtful frown, ' but whether it was St Mary's, I'm afraid I've no idea.'

She noticed the tell-tale blankness stealing across his face, and added, ' If you really want to know, someone who might tell you is the vicar. I hear he's quite knowledgeable about local history. Would you like to go and ask him ? '

Colin nodded dumbly.

' Very well, then,' said Miss Seymour decisively. She took some notepaper and an envelope from her desk and began to scribble rapidly. ' You should find him in the church or his vicarage on most evenings, I suppose. I'll give you a note explaining that I've sent you : then he'll be more likely to help.'

Colin managed somehow to conceal his excitement ;

69

but he could hardly keep from hugging himself as he realized how far this unexpected slice of luck might take them.

'There you are,' said the teacher, folding the letter and sealing it inside the envelope. 'That should do the trick. Now off you go; I must get this marking finished before midnight!'

'Thank you, Miss,' mumbled Colin shyly, pushing the letter into his pocket.

'That's all right,' replied Miss Seymour, taking up her red pencil once more. Then her blue eyes turned on him disconcertingly and she added, 'I don't know what you're up to, Colin. But I'm sure you're quite aware that *mischief* and history don't mix.'

Colin blinked.

'Yes, Miss,' he muttered, his cheeks reddening. She didn't answer; her pencil was poised over the first English exercise, and Colin scuttled in relief for the door.

As he opened it, he seemed for an instant to see a shadow slither round the bend at the far end of the corridor. Puzzled, for surely everyone else should have left ages ago, he concluded it must have been a trick of the light streaming from the classroom. He groped behind him to close its door, and, as his fingers closed on the handle, discovered that it was strangely warm.

On a shrewd impulse he ran to the Games cupboard half-way down the passage, and clambered up till he could see through the high window above. He was just in time to see Victor Brooksbank sprinting out through the school gates and down the street as though a pack of wolves was at his heels.

Colin met Roy on the corner immediately after tea as they had arranged, and dragged him off at a brisk pace down the High Street. For a change, it was not his but Roy's legs that found it difficult to keep up.

Passing the last of the shops, they slowed down on the river bridge and paused for breath. Leaning over the parapet, they watched the green water oozing below, its ripples occasionally flattened by gusts of cold, spring wind.

'I wish this church business'd keep!' muttered Roy grimly.

'Why—don't you want to come?' asked Colin, startled.

'Was hoping we'd clean out the hut tonight,' explained the older boy disconsolately. 'We said we'd do it last Saturday, but we ended up at Boulton's.'

'There's no hurry,' said Colin. 'It'll still be there tomorrow.'

'So will the church,' retorted Roy.

Colin grimaced at the patterned water, feeling mildly exasperated. He wondered whether Mrs Smithson would be as gloomy as her son, once she knew they were after an amount that could send the whole family on holiday ten times over. Then he told himself realistically that Mrs Smithson—or any other grown-up for that matter—would be much more likely to laugh at their whole story.

'Why *shouldn't* Kemp have hidden his silver in the steeple?' he remarked defensively. 'Perhaps—perhaps on the rafters, or in some sort of cubby-hole?'

Roy grunted non-committally.

Colin produced the snuff-box lid from his coat pocket, and laid it on the stone wall under his friend's nose.

'Tell me another reason why he mentions the steeple in the first line?' he challenged.

Roy was silent. Encouraged, Colin went on, 'And those last two lines,

With threaded needle
Is silver sown,

must mean Kemp stitched it up inside something, like a sack or a canvas bag. Anyway, that's the sort of thing we'll have to search for.'

'*If* he hid it there, and *if* it's the same steeple Kemp meant,' said Roy moodily. He pushed himself off the parapet with one thrust of his lean arms, and walked on across the bridge. 'Come on. The sooner we get this bug out of your system, the better.'

On the opposite bank from the shopping centre sprawled the old village from which modern Wheatleigh had grown; and it was only a ten-minute walk from the river to St Mary's church. Its great clock said just after six as Colin pushed open the worn iron gate, and stepped cautiously into the churchyard.

Black, lop-sided gravestones edged the gravel path winding to the church. Colin kept warily to the centre and trained his eyes on the clock-tower ahead.

Fashioned from dark-grey, granite blocks, it climbed to sixty feet above the door in its base ; and then just over the stark whiteness of the clock, began the six-sided spire, mounting into the sky like a giant's javelin.

It looked taller and somehow menacing from so near at hand. Feeling shrunken and dizzy, Colin forced his eyes up to the famous weather-vane on its tip, the silhouette of a smocked farmer wielding a scythe, who swung round with the wind inside a great hoop six feet across ; Miss Seymour had once told them it had been photographed for a book all about unusual weather-vanes.

As they neared the foot of the tower, Colin blinked his eyes back to earth, and gathered his wits.

The clack of his shoes in the porchway was disconcertingly loud. Ill at ease, Roy waited on the path while he tried the latch on the iron-studded door. It was almost a relief to discover it was locked.

' Good ! ' declared Roy feelingly, churning his feet round in the gravel. ' And we've still time to do the hut.' He began to stalk towards the gate.

Colin did not move. He had just noticed a wooden plaque nailed beside the church door.

Roy halted irritably. ' What's that you've found ? " This Week's Weddings " ? ' he asked.

Colin shook his head. ' This *was* the steeple,' he declared simply.

Roy returned and peered at the neat, yellow lettering.

This Church of St Mary was founded by the generosity and piety of Sir Grenfell Kemp, landowner and squire in Wheatleigh for three decades until his death in 1781. He bequeathed certain monies " to be applied towards the building or other uses and services of a Church or Chapel-of-Ease in the Borough of Wheatleigh."

This present site was approved in 1785 by the Parliamentary Commissioners for the Building of Churches.

The foundation stone was laid in 1787 by Sir Grenfell's son, Leonard Kemp, and the completed Church was consecrated in 1790 by the Bishop of Winchester. Leonard Kemp died in 1812, but the founder's grandson, Charles Nathaniel Kemp, continued his family's services to this Church by fulfilling the post of Church-Elder from 1815 till his untimely death in 1830.

This was followed by a string of details about the church's architecture ; but Roy had read enough.

' All right,' he said grudgingly, ' it probably is the one he meant. So what ? You've still got to——'

He stopped. Colin followed the direction of his gaze. Watching them from the gate, his black gown writhing in the wind, was the Reverend James Greenhale.

Colin had seen the parson once before, in March, when the clergyman had visited Barnsley Road School for a talk with Mr Hull. Whether it had been to make a complaint or merely to conduct routine business, Colin did not know ; but the parson's square, iron-like jaw, acid eyes and grim bearing had not spoken of someone over-fond of boys.

Mustering his courage, Colin led the way up the path.

The parson was waiting for them at the gate, and the suspicious glint behind his spectacles made Colin very thankful for the protective letter in his pocket.

' And what are you boys doing here ? '

The voice was cold and unwelcoming.

Colin managed to speak up more confidently than

he felt. 'Please, sir—I've brought this letter for you.'

The parson took it in his loose-skinned hand, and opened it silently. Roy tossed the sheaf of hair out of his eyes, and scowled at the gravel between his feet.

The boys waited for what seemed an age; and when at last the clergyman began to fold the letter up very deliberately, his look seemed scarcely less frigid.

'According to Miss Seymour,' he declared slowly, putting the letter into the jacket pocket beneath his robe, 'one of you boys is interested in the history of my church.'

'She means me, sir,' uttered Colin.

'And your name is—?'

'Colin Trant, sir.'

The parson gathered in his billowing gown once more, and eyed him piercingly.

'I thought boys of your age were only interested in getting themselves into mischief,' he remarked dryly. 'What's your friend's name?'

'Roy Smithson, sir,' said Colin, wishing his companion would raise his eyes and not look so surly.

'What's this question your teacher mentions?'

Colin paused warily; now they knew the age of the church, he could use this opportunity in other directions.

'Well, sir—we—we were rather interested in the steeple.' He nodded lamely at the spire soaring up before them.

The parson frowned in puzzlement for a moment; then his brow cleared.

'I suppose you mean the origin of the weather-vane ?' he demanded. 'Hasn't your teacher told you ?'

'N—no, sir.' Colin was rather taken aback by the parson's misunderstanding. He tried to lead him on to better ground. 'I meant the steeple itsel——'

'Don't you know why it's a farmer carrying a scythe ?' interrupted the clergyman, waving Colin to silence with a large, decisive hand.

In an effort to escape those frowning eyes, Colin shook his head dumbly and looked inquiringly at Roy ; but the older boy just grimaced.

'Heavens, boy—isn't it obvious ?' snorted the man in sudden impatience. 'A hundred years ago the farmers here grew almost nothing but wheat, of course. Why else should they call this place Wheatleigh ? Now, tell me why the farmer's got an iron hoop all round him.'

'I—I've no idea, sir,' Colin stammered.

'The wheat won't ripen unless there's sunshine,' went on the parson grimly, 'so the hoop is supposed to represent the sun.'

Colin nodded politely. There was an abrupt silence.

'Well, is that all ?' demanded the clergyman suddenly. He frowned up at the clock.

Colin licked his lips. The steeple . . . he must ask some sort of question about the steeple . . . He shut out the soft, meaningful cough that Roy gave. One more try.

'Please, sir, aren't—aren't those bricks newer than the rest ?' he blurted, pointing to where the clock-

77

tower met the eaves of the spire. He had first noticed the extra light colour of the top stonework when Roy and he had arrived earlier ; it seemed as good a gambit as any to get the parson on to the right subject.

The evening light glistened on the clergyman's spectacles as he followed the direction of Colin's finger.

' Correct,' he grunted. ' The steeple was condemned as dangerous in 1934, so it had to be rebuilt. That makes those bricks nearly a hundred and fifty years younger than all the rest . . . Pity ! '

Just then the clock began to strike half past. The vicar exclaimed with annoyance.

' I shall be late. Off you go, boys. Shut the gate after you.' He set off down the path, his robe streaming like a long black mane.

With a hiss of pent-up irritation, Roy slouched out through the gateway on to the pavement. For a second, Colin did not move ; then sudden dread shot through him, and he sprinted after the clergyman.

' Please, sir—when—when the workmen re—rebuilt the steeple,' he panted, falling into step beside him, ' did—did they find anything interesting ? '

Without slackening his stride, the parson regarded him shrewdly ; what might have been a glimmer of amusement appeared in his eyes.

' You're thinking of skeletons, long-lost manuscripts and priest-holes ? ' he conjectured dryly. ' Then I shall have to disappoint you. All they found were the remains of a game of cricket.'

Colin stared.

'Some dead bats,' explained the parson, giving the ghost of a smile. By now they had reached the porchway, and he added, 'If you boys were a little fonder of reading, you'd have saved the time of both of us.'

His broad finger stabbed lower down the plaque Colin had been reading before. It was a short paragraph by itself.

In 1934 *the spire and upper stages of the tower were condemned as dangerous, through the crumbling and bad weathering of the stone. The overall cost of rebuilding, together with the installation of a fine new tenor bell, amounted to over £1700.*

Colin felt as if the ground beneath him had turned into a cruel whirlpool.

The clergyman paused in the doorway and frowned at him thoughtfully. For a moment his gaze almost seemed to soften.

'It's a pleasant surprise to meet a boy keen on history,' he declared, pulling back the edge of his gown and reaching in an inside pocket. 'Here's a ticket for a lecture you might care to attend ; it deals with the Enclosure Movement of the last century. It's at the Town Hall in a few weeks' time. If you can come, you'll hear quite a lot about Wheatleigh.'

He thrust a printed card into Colin's hand, nodded curtly, and disappeared into the church.

Only when they reached the bridge did Roy end the simmering truce between them.

'Decided how we're going to waste *tomorrow* night yet?'

His voice was thick with frustration.

'I couldn't stop him lecturing, could I?' burst out Colin angrily. 'And it was as good a place to look as anywhere else. You should be glad Kemp *didn't* hide it there, or the workmen would have found it.'

'Oh, sure!' sneered Roy. 'Kemp hid it specially for *you* to find, didn't he? Well, where're you going to look now? We've seen his "steeple"; and there aren't any "yonder grindstones"; you're only left with "threaded needles". I suppose you'll suggest we start doing needlework now?'

'Oh, don't talk so stupid!' retorted Colin, goaded into losing his temper.

'*Me* stupid?' snarled Roy. He tossed his hair back furiously. 'You're the stupid one here—expecting to find something lost more'n a hundred years ago, and worrying yourself silly over a crazy poem! Then dragging me here to listen to that old fool blathering away for half an hour, when we could've been doing the hut!' Viciously he snatched a handful of leaves from the hedge they were passing, then turned on Colin abruptly. 'Look, I've had enough! If you want to keep on wasting your time and making a fool of yourself, you can do: but count me out!'

His face dark with passion, he spun round and sprinted swiftly up the street.

Listlessly Colin watched him go.

8

A Threat

By the middle of May the Old Field had shown its summer clothes in earnest. The scattered elders were frothed in white. Clumps of ragged robin thronged crimson in the hollows. Thistles and buttercups lifted their proud colours above the grass, and the sweet air hummed with bees and midges.

The very colour made everything more difficult to paint. Now that the new conservatory had been glazed and varnished, and Tim's pram triumphantly installed, Colin was able to labour over his sketch-book on most evenings of the week ; and it was only then, squatting on the hillock he had found for himself in February, that he fully understood how his paint-brush was indeed his worst enemy. No matter how he tried, time and again he would turn a painstaking pencil-drawing into a coloured jigsaw, a mosaic without depth or coherence —as though each separate object were trying to prove itself more important than its neighbour.

It was a hot Saturday afternoon, with hardly three weeks left to the closing date of the competition, when his frustration came to a head. Perhaps too much striving had made him stale, or the sultry weather had dulled his spirits ; whatever the reason, by the time the steeple clock struck four, he was thoroughly glad to rinse his brush in the jar of grey water beside him, and snap it away inside his paint-box.

He held the sketch-book at arm's length, and eyed the still-damp painting cynically ; it was no better than last week's attempts—certainly nowhere near good enough to win a competition.

He lowered the book and gazed at the glittering stream nearby. He was almost beginning to detest it, along with all the other things he couldn't colour properly on paper—the bramble patches, the yellow-beaded furze, the mossy ridges marking the old sunken walls. For an instant his eyes even lingered on the screen of hawthorns in the far corner. Then he shrugged indifferently ; the hut had been dead ever since Roy had walked out on him.

He should have asked the parson better questions that evening, Colin told himself, swiftly changing his thoughts. Perhaps those builders had lied ; perhaps they had found the silver after all, when they'd erected the new steeple. In that case, he could stop worrying ; but if not ? Suppose Kemp's hoard were still waiting to be discovered ?

Resolutely he slipped the paint-box into his pocket. For a start, there must be several other buildings in Wheatleigh dating from before the Labourers' Revolt ; he could find out which they were, and investigate them. Maybe one had even housed a grindstone.

A grindstone. *Marry the steeple to yonder grindstone.* Colin had a second idea. If ' marry ' was an archaic word for 'unite', might not 'grindstone' have another meaning? For instance, it wasn't very different from '*grave*stone', was it? There were acres of those in St Mary's churchyard, under the steeple's very nose, so to speak.

Automatically he began to raise his eyes towards the spire—and then stopped: something had suddenly moved beyond the clay slope, scuttling behind the hazels as if not wanting to be seen.

Knowing that on top of the hillock he himself was in full view, Colin casually collected up his painting things and descended the slope in the direction of the hole in the fence. Once out of sight, he veered rapidly to the left and began to make his way round, using every scrap of cover he could find.

He reached the slope to the lower field at a spot close to the factory wall, and was just in time to see someone disappear behind the hawthorn copse. Scrambling down the steep bank, Colin sprinted frantically, throwing caution to the winds, and burst out above the hut just as Victor Brooksbank was tugging aside its iron door.

'You can leave that alone, and clear out!' he rapped, striding down into the hollow.

The ginger-headed boy spun round guiltily. 'Oh—it's you,' he muttered; he grinned in an attempt at friendliness, but nevertheless released the iron promptly. 'Now you and Smithson've fallen out and don't use this place, I thought I might as well take over.'

'Then you'd better think again!' snapped Colin,

hiding his surprise. Now, how had Brooksbank found *that* out? More snooping, probably; he was quite good at it, Colin knew from past experience. 'We're moving back in tomorrow,' he lied; and then added dryly, 'and we don't fancy taking over a thief's kitchen.'

Brooksbank scowled. 'You calling me names?' he rasped.

'Remember that pencil-case?' asked Colin pointedly. 'By the way, learnt to draw with it yet?'

The other's cheeks went the colour of flour, and his plump hands curled into fists. Colin pretended not to notice, and pushed the corrugated iron back into place, while bracing himself inwardly.

But even that was unnecessary; for after one tense second, Brooksbank suddenly turned and stalked off up the bank of the hollow.

Reaching the hawthorns, he hesitated, then muttered maliciously over his shoulder.

'You and Smithson think you're on to something, don't you? You'll be laughing the other side of your faces before long, when I beat you to it.'

At a steady trot, he vanished among the elder trees, leaving Colin startled and motionless beside the hut.

Colin hurried his tea as much as his mother's insistence on table-manners would allow, and then made a prompt escape towards the High Street.

It was still busy with shoppers, although as it was almost half past five, the worst of the Saturday afternoon crush must have ebbed. There was a crowd as usual

84

trying to establish a bridgehead on the zebra-crossing, but just as Colin arrived, an obliging bus-driver halted, and he was able to get across without any loss of time.

There being no shops on the other side, it was easier going.

The fourth turning on the left, Roy had once told him. He counted three rather dreary-looking streets opening off from the main road, and stopped at the next. Its name-plate, high on the side of an old boot-repairing shop, was too shabby to read ; but it did not matter, for at the far end Colin recognized the spiked railings Roy had once mentioned. Beyond them swirled the river.

In Bravender Place the front doors opened straight on to the pavement, and as Colin walked along, snatches of music and voices accompanied him down the street. Most of the houses seemed tuned in to a crime serial on television ; a mere half-dozen preferred a children's concert on the radio. Even the insides seemed determined to be alike, thought Colin.

He had to cross over for the even numbers. Number 62 was not quite half-way down, a dull, narrow-fronted affair.

He knocked, trying to fight down a sudden nervousness. There was a game of hopscotch chalked on the uneven pavement.

From inside came the crying of a baby, followed by hurried footsteps and the clatter of a bucket. Then the wailing stopped, and a moment later the door was opened by a woman holding a small child. Her hands were glistening with soapy water, and drops spattered on her apron as she tried to tug the baby's shawl farther up round its head, to keep off the cold wind.

As Colin asked his question, he realized how much like Roy she looked. Yet her face seemed more weary and gaunt, though that, he told himself, might have been simply the effect of the gloom in the passage.

'No, love, he's at the warehouse,' she replied. 'His Uncle Phil's on late shift tonight and Roy's gone to help wash the van or something.'

'When—when'll he be back?' ventured Colin.

'Seven; he said he'd bath Janet—that's this one—' she smiled down fondly, 'while I tackle her sister Annie. He can be a real blessing at times. You're his pal Colin, aren't you?'

He nodded.

'I thought so. Well, that's where you'll find him, Colin. You know where it is, don't you?'

'Yes. Thanks—thanks a lot,' he stammered eagerly. She smiled and then hurried inside.

Some weeks after edging perilously along its 'Tightrope', Colin had discovered that Rimmington's had a more orthodox approach: a secondary road branching off the High Street. Half-walking, half-running now that the shops were shut and the pavements clearer, he arrived there in record time, breathless and worried.

Passing the office entrance with its black and gold name-plate, he sauntered hopefully round to the yard at the side. To his relief he saw that the late shift had not yet ended: the main gates were open, and so too

87

were the garage doors across the concreted yard. Parked before them were two vans, being loaded with assorted boxes and bundles of paper by men in overalls.

All at once he spotted Roy, who was crouching down officiously beside one of the van wheels, looking as if he were testing tyre-pressures.

Mustering his courage, Colin whistled cautiously.

No one seemed to hear. Roy had found a real or imaginary rust-mark and had begun to polish the hub with a piece of rag.

Colin tried again louder. That was better ; the dark-haired boy paused and looked round, then stared at Colin in angry surprise. He grimaced as the other waved him over, and at first did not move ; in fact, it was only when Colin's beckoning grew frantic and brought curious glances from the workmen, that he reluctantly pocketed his duster and drifted to the gate.

' Well, what's up, then ? ' he muttered, adding sourly, ' Found Kemp's silver, I suppose.'

It was a gibe Colin had anticipated.

' I might have done, for all you know,' he countered. ' Still think it can't be found, do you ? '

' Do Eskimos live in Egypt ? ' said Roy.

They eyed each other like wary fencers. Colin changed his tactics.

' Be a sport, Roy—give it one more try ! ' he urged.

' What for ? ' Roy shrugged his shoulders ; he was more interested in a passing lorry.

' What for ? ' groaned Colin, in sudden exasperation. ' You mean you're quite happy just to sit back and do nothing, and see it taken from right under our noses ? '

Roy looked at him.

' Mean there's someone else after it, then ? ' he asked sharply.

Colin nodded.

' Victor Brooksbank,' he said, and went on to describe the veiled threat that had been made at the Old Field that afternoon.

Roy listened, stony-faced, and then shook his head dubiously.

' How *could* he know what you're after ? ' he growled suddenly. ' He means something else, I bet. You've just got old Kemp on the brain.'

' Brooksbank's in my class at school, don't forget,' persisted Colin, doing his best to keep his temper. ' He heard that lesson all about the lost silver, just as I did. And—and there's something else, too ! ' he blurted, suddenly remembering.

' What ? '

' That afternoon I stopped behind at school—you know, to ask Miss Seymour if the steeple went back to Kemp's day—well, I spotted Brooksbank scampering off afterwards and I'm pretty sure he'd been listening outside the door. That would've told him a lot ! '

Roy was silent for a moment. Colin had disquieted him, but he found it hard to jettison his stubbornness.

' Look—if we join forces again,' continued Colin earnestly, ' we're bound to find it first. Two of us could easily work quicker than him ; and besides, we've got Kemp's verse to go on.'

'I'd be more convinced,' snorted Roy, half-serious, half-cynical, 'if you'd managed to turn that poem into some sort of sense—or—or found a fresh clue, or something.'

There was a take-it-or-leave-it tone in his voice, and Colin realized that however long he preached, Roy would not be persuaded that evening : not argument, but concrete proof, was what the older boy needed in his present mood.

The realization made Colin stare hopelessly across the yard. And it was then that he saw it.

Some trick of the fading sunlight must have been responsible, for he'd looked in that direction several times before. But only at that instant did its meaning burst upon his mind, like manna from heaven.

'Matter of fact, I *have* got a fresh clue,' he stammered swiftly.

Roy's eyes narrowed.

'What is it, then ? '

Mastering his excitement, Colin realized he could use his discovery in more ways than one.

'Didn't think you'd be interested ! ' he blurted in feigned surprise.

'Depends what it is. Anyway, don't let's argue. What've you found ? '

Colin wandered indifferently to the edge of the pavement, and looked towards the deserted High Street.

'It'd be a waste of breath telling you,' he declared serenely. 'You said yourself the silver'd never be discovered.'

Roy's hands screwed themselves up into impatient, exasperated knots, and then opened feebly.

'Look! Let's hear it and get it over with!' he snorted. 'And—and I'll come in with you again, if that's what you're after.'

'Friends again?' urged Colin promptly.

'All right—friends again,' agreed Roy. They shook hands, the one perfunctorily, the other ardently. 'Now, out with it—before I throttle you!'

Colin swallowed with relief; the friendship was patched up—in a fashion. Now to business.

'Look over there,' he ordered eagerly, pointing over the other's shoulder.

Roy turned and followed the direction of his finger.

In the far corner of Rimmington's yard lay a great hillock of rubble—shattered bricks, rotting wood, broken drain-pipes and guttering, mostly overgrown with weeds and coarse grass. It looked as if builders had at some time made vast alterations inside the printing office, and had piled all their debris there.

Leaning against the wall, half-smothered by it all, was the cause of Colin's elation—a five-foot granite grindstone.

9

' . . . To Yonder Grindstone '

The church clock glowed in the darkening sky, like a bright round hole in some plush curtains. It said ten to nine as the two boys left the hut at last and picked their way carefully across the Old Field towards the hole in the fence.

' We could've left half an hour ago,' muttered Roy peevishly, when they reached the long, flat ridge with the willow on its crest just visible through the gloom. ' I told you, last shift always ends at half past eight.'

' And I told you, it won't be dark enough before nine,' retorted Colin, equally nervy. He flashed his torch to avoid some thistles as they neared the fence, and a moment later squeezed cautiously out into the street.

Neither of them spoke again till they emerged some minutes later on to the brightly lit main road.

' You're sure about this nightwatchman, are you ? demanded Colin suddenly, as they turned down towards the river.

' Uncle Phil reckons he hardly stirs from the boss's office,' said Roy. ' Suppose he must look into the warehouse and workshops once or twice, but I can't see him ever visiting the yard.'

'Is it any good asking *him* if we can dig out the grindstone?'

Roy shrugged.

'You heard what my uncle told us,' he grunted. 'This night-chap might be even more fussy.'

Colin nodded. 'At least, this way'll save us awkward questions,' he commented wryly.

Once through the shopping-centre, they reached the turning leading to the printer's; and Colin saw outlined against the purple sky the great peaked roof he had drawn so often; from here it was hard to believe that its far, windowless wall fell sheer into the river, which was now completely masked by buildings.

'Funny how you saw it straight off, and here's me been helping at the garage five nights a week,' murmured Roy thoughtfully.

'I suppose you couldn't see the wood for the trees,' said Colin, using his mother's favourite expression.

As they drew near the broad garage gates, they stepped more softly. The nearest street-lamp was a good thirty yards away, throwing only the faintest of glimmers on to the stout padlock.

Colin stopped and glanced up and down the street. All clear, as far as you could tell in that light.

'You first?' he muttered. 'You know it best.'

Filling his lungs, Roy crouched like a cat, and then sprang. For an instant he hung by his arms, while his shoes thudded and scrambled at the stout boards. Then his foot found the padlock, he thrust himself upward and leaned breathless across the gate top.

93

'All right?' Colin's voice floated up anxiously from below.

'Nearly there,' gasped Roy. Kicking off strongly from the lock, he threw one leg over the gate, lay for a moment face-downward along its length, then swiftly let himself down the other side.

The garage yard sprawled before him, as black and still as the bottom of a well. 'Come on,' he croaked eagerly.

It wasn't quite so easy for short-limbed Colin; he had to leap three times before getting sufficient grip on the gate top, and was well out of both breath and buoyancy when he slithered down to his friend one nerve-racked minute later.

For a second they crouched motionless, wincing at the echo of his shoes on the concrete. But the windows of the warehouse remained black and silent, and at length Colin switched on his torch.

On the right rose the broad cliff of the building, the garage doors in its base closed like a sleeper's eyelids. The rest of the yard was enclosed by a high wall, over which drifted the sound of the river just beyond. Roy realized it was the first time he had heard its murmuring from there: the yard was too busy during the day.

Moving as quietly as possible, they approached the bank of rubble piled against the far wall, where the grindstone was half-buried. Tensely Colin played his torch over it. It looked more massive than ever in that unreal light; he judged that its worn, chipped rim reached a good foot above his head.

Surely it must be the one Kemp had meant; Colin just couldn't bring himself to believe in any more set-backs. There *had* to be another clue carved on its gnarled surface : a map or perhaps an arrow. He did not dare hope that the silver collection itself might be there, in several tightly stitched leathern bags.

Bringing himself down to earth with a struggle, Colin reminded himself that their first task was to discover whether the grindstone was old enough.

' Think that bit o' wood'll suit you ? ' whispered Roy. He pointed to a broken board half-way up the mound.

Colin wrenched it out ; in parts it was somewhat splintery, but sound enough to make a shovel of sorts.

' An' I'll use this,' continued the taller boy, working loose a twisted piece of iron.

They tackled the heap close to the wall, with the torch propped on a loose brick beside them. A mere five minutes were enough to convince Colin that the rubble alone was sufficiently old : the tough tangle of weed-roots could hardly have sprung up in much less than a thousand years ! Fiercely he stabbed his make-shift spade into the bank, working loose its spongy crust of moss and wild grasses.

Crouched beside him, Roy steadily shovelled the freed earth and stones out of the way ; but the deeper Colin progressed, more and more often Roy's iron had to be reversed and used as a lever on the heavier obstacles—beams, lumps of concrete and cracked flag-stones.

Long before they had exposed the nearest rim of the

grindstone, the sweat was trickling down Colin's arms. The rough edges of his shovel had brought sore, red lines across his palms, and by the time they reached the axle-hole, he was only too glad to pause and see whether they had uncovered any carving yet.

The smooth granite, however, bore no marks so far, except for one or two lumps chipped out by the rubble flung over it ; and getting their breath once more, the two boys continued their assault.

Ten minutes' arm-wrenching effort brought them to the final core of bricks and concrete slabs. In weary relief, these were half-kicked, half-dragged clear, and then came the eager, scrambling search with the torch.

The worn, grey surface was quite blank.

The two boys looked at each other. Numb with dismay, Colin battled to make himself think.

' There—there could be something on the back—facing the wall,' he blurted after a moment's pause.

He saw Roy's eyes swing dispiritedly back to the grindstone.

' An' how the devil're you going to shift that ? ' uttered the elder boy hoarsely, thrusting back the dark hair tumbled across his forehead.

Colin nodded at the gap behind. ' I'm the smallest —I'll—I'll squeeze in and have a look. You hold the torch.'

Swallowing hard, Roy directed the beam into the narrow gap between the wall and the leaning granite, while Colin dragged aside several loose bricks and timbers. Then the younger boy set his back against

the brickwork and began to work himself sideways into the space.

It was a tight fit. He scraped his skull painfully against the rough wall, before managing to double up small enough. Laboriously he shuffled almost to the centre.

' The torch,' he panted.

He felt Roy's thin fingers press it into his hand. Twisting his head as best he could, he manoeuvred the disc of light slowly round the back of the grindstone. Once. Twice. Three times.

' Well, for pity's sake, say *something* ! ' burst out Roy.

Colin felt sudden misery welling up inside him. ' There's nothing here,' he replied dully.

' There must be ! Look again,' urged Roy in frantic disbelief. ' A—a sign ; a number . . . Anything . . . '

Laboriously Colin played the yellow light once more over every inch of the great stone circle. He knew full well it would be wasted effort : the same worn, smooth surface all the way from top to——

A shiver of joy pricked his spine. There on the very edge, at the place where his cramped foot had just been resting, he could see some tiny figures cut into the granite.

Hunching himself lower still, he steadied the torch and read them. For a moment he was quite still, while he digested their meaning ; then he was shuffling eagerly sideways once more, scrambling to get out.

He was just about to thrust his shoulders free and gasp out his news, when he suddenly felt Roy seize his exposed wrist, tear the torch from his grasp and plunge them into darkness.

'What d'you think you're playing at?' blurted Colin in exasperation. 'Put it on ag——'

'Shut up!' hissed Roy, frantically. 'Nightwatch-man's coming!'

Colin froze.

All at once came the sharp creak of a door, followed by the stutter of Roy's shoes racing for the gate. A beam of light sliced out from the direction of the garage doors, swung erratically for a moment, then veered towards the sound of feet scrabbling on wood.

'Huh! Might've known it'd be a blame boy!' The voice choked over its mixture of relief and rage. '*Come back, you young imp!*'

Crouched behind the grindstone, Colin heard the answer: the clump of shoes beyond the gate, and the patter as they raced off along the pavement.

'Wait till I tell your uncle, Roy Smithson!' bellowed the nightwatchman caustically.

The sound of Roy's flight dwindled swiftly into nothingness. There was a moment's silence, save for the even murmur of the river. Then slowly that powerful beam moved round the yard.

Feeling sick, Colin watched it sweep towards the scattered rubble; he closed his eyes, and cringed still farther behind the broad stone circle.

He heard the man swear at the sight of the mess.

''E or 'is uncle'll clear that little lot up,' came the sour mumble, ''cos I shan't, for sure.'

For two long minutes, the torchlight glared round the grindstone. Colin's every muscle felt taut as a bowstring ; he could only pray that none of him was sticking into view, and that the man would come no nearer.

There was a sudden click, and the light went out. A door whined shut, and in a sweat of relief, Colin realized he'd escaped.

It demanded all his nerve to stop himself from sprinting for the gate, there and then. He forced himself to count to a hundred, and give the nightwatchman time to settle down again in the office.

It turned out to be a very quick hundred. In fact, he reached the safety of the High Street less than three minutes later.

On Sunday afternoon Colin arrived at the Old Field determined to tackle at last the cleaning of the hut. Now that the breach between them was healed, with Roy receiving the worst end of the grindstone affair, Colin felt that carrying out his friend's old suggestion was the least he could do.

Under his arm, wrapped in his plastic mac, was Mrs Trant's smallest carpet-brush. He had managed to smuggle it out while his mother was spooning sieved greens into Tim's ever-open mouth ; and the weather being duller today, no questions had been asked when he had left home with the innocent-seeming bundle in his hand.

He found the hut snugger than ever, behind its new

white-speckled shield of hawthorn blossom. First of all, he brushed down its walls, taking care not to loosen their laboriously built jigsaws of tin, stones and plywood ; this made short shrift of at least a score of cobwebs that spread out like grey skirts towards the grassy bank. Then, standing on tip-toe, he swept the roofing-felt free of twigs and grit ; it crackled a little under the brush, just as when his father had first removed it from the old greenhouse during their spring-cleaning. Colin wondered whether *this* would be called summer-cleaning.

He next tackled the inside of the hut. Spasmodically over the months, they had furnished it, after a fashion. As well as a packing-case for a table and the apple-box and oil-drum for chairs, there was also a well-worn oblong of lino (from Roy's rag-and-bone man) on the ground, and a shelf nailed on to the sunken wall—a further example of Roy's ingenuity. Those things that could be moved, Colin carried outside and gave a stiff brushing all over, topside and bottom. Several earwigs and spiders scurried from the packing-case, and there was an even more unpleasant collection under the linoleum. But it all served to make Colin feel the more virtuous and satisfied.

He had just put everything back and was musing whether to start another painting, when he heard the sudden swish of hawthorn branches, and a moment later Roy came slouching into the hollow.

The way he flopped wearily on to the grass, without a glance at the hut, told Colin a great deal.

'Get into trouble?' he asked, squatting down alongside.

'Uncle Phil called on us on his way home,' grunted Roy.

Colin grimaced, and returned the sketch-book to his pocket.

'What did he say?'

'Nothing: 's what he did that hurt,' was the retort. Uncle Phil, Colin knew, had large brawny hands, fashioned by long years at the driving wheel.

'Didn't think I'd be able to sit down as soon as this,' went on the older boy with a rueful grin. 'Though he said it wasn't a quarter of what I'd get next time. Then went on about better spend my weekends earning some money to help Mum out.' He sighed, then added indifferently, 'We could do a lot worse, I suppose.'

Colin frowned.

'How's that?' he asked abruptly, rolling over on to his stomach and plucking a tall grass stem.

Roy shrugged. 'Turned out a waste of time, last night, didn't it?' he commented sourly.

Colin removed the stalk from his mouth as if it were the stem of a pipe. 'Not exactly,' he said.

Roy stared at him hard; then spotted the queer gleam in his eyes.

'Go on,' he ordered suspiciously.

Colin sat up, unable to suppress his excitement any longer.

'Just before you had to run for it, I found a date carved on the grindstone: 1823.'

There was a thoughtful silence. 'So it *is* old enough,' muttered Roy at length.

Colin nodded.

'I've been trying to work out the next step,' he blurted. 'You got any ideas on it?'

'Well, I've been thinking a bit about that verse,' admitted Roy slowly. 'Got Kemp's lid on you, have you?'

'Should have,' murmured Colin, feeling in his jacket pocket. 'Anyway, go on.'

'You know that part about the threaded needle?' continued Roy, somewhat reluctantly. 'And how we've been thinking his silver must be stitched up in a sack or a leather bag?'

'Well?' said Colin, trying another pocket.

'Why couldn't he have stitched it up inside his saddle?' concluded Roy tersely.

Colin blinked.

'Pretty hard for sitting on,' he commented dryly.

'It fits in with the story, though,' argued Roy, sitting bolt-upright. 'You said that when they set fire to his manor house, he made a dash for the stables: why not with the idea of saving his silver as well as himself?'

Colin grunted doubtfully.

'It's a good try, Roy,' he admitted, 'but you couldn't hide huge things like dishes and vases and goblets there, could you?'

As the older boy lay back nonplussed on the grass, Colin stood up and groped down each of his trouser pockets; his brow gathered into a frown.

'Just when you specially want something,' he declared, ' it starts playing hide-and-seek with you.'

He began to turn out his pockets, stacking their contents at the foot of the corrugated-iron door. There were several things he didn't know he had, like some cigarette cards and a dozen or so screws—Must be getting like Dad ! he told himself—but there was no snuff-box lid.

' When did you look at it last ? ' said Roy, sitting up again.

Colin frowned.

' I think it was last Thursday, coming home from school. I was going through ideas about the steeple part, and I took it out to see if any of them'd fit. And then——' All at once he grinned triumphantly. ' I know ! It was drizzling ; I must have put it in my mac pocket instead ! '

Darting into the hut, he rescued the rolled-up rain-coat from the packing-case table. He opened it out, somehow managing to ignore Roy's hoots of laughter as the carpet-brush made a surprise re-appearance. The plastic was creased and stuck together, and it took Colin some impatient fumbling to penetrate into the pockets. There was only an old bus-ticket in the left-hand one, so the lid would be in the . . .

His hand went limp.

' It's not there,' he muttered dully.

' Bet you pulled it out with your hankie, and never heard it drop ! ' suggested Roy.

Reluctantly Colin nodded ; he'd done that sort of

thing before; those pockets were slippery as well as shallow. He was upset, not so much at losing Kemp's verse, which he felt he now knew by heart, as at losing their only link with the Kemp story itself; the snuff-box lid had been something tangible, reassuringly solid, and now that it had gone, it was much harder to believe that the events of 1830 had really happened. He found himself murmuring the verse, ruefully.

> *Marry the steeple*
> *To yonder grindstone.*
> *With threaded needle*
> *Is silver sown.*

'Got another idea about Rimmington's grindstone, then?' grunted Roy.

Colin grimaced. 'It's not much. I just thought we might get a bit further if we could find out how it came to be in that yard, that's all.'

Roy watched him begin returning the articles to his pockets one by one.

'How're you going to do that?' asked the older boy. 'Tackle Miss Seymour again?'

'Could do, I suppose,' muttered Colin. The strain of his last 'audience' with her was still raw in his memory; in addition, it was such an obscure piece of information he was after, that he knew instinctively it wouldn't be in her possession. 'A specialist in local history's what we really want.'

'Not the parson again!' groaned Roy. 'Whatsis-name Greenhorn—we'd get another lecture on old weather-vanes!'

'His name's Greenhale,' grinned Colin, crouching to put the last few things back into his pocket. He'd quite forgotten that the vicar of St Mary's was also an historian ; not that *his* kind of history would be likely to include stray grindstones either ; still, if there was no one else to ask, then they'd——

He stopped, his hand poised over the very last of his possessions, his heart thumping madly.

Their problem was solved.

'I—I know who we'll ask,' he stammered huskily, recovering himself.

'Old Hully ?' guessed Roy.

Colin's hand descended and gripped the printed card lying on the grass.

'No. "Professor Dorothy Greaves of Bristol University,"' he read out boldly.

It took Roy several seconds to recognize the parson's invitation to the local history lecture.

'But—but it's in school time !' he blurted, thunderstruck. 'We said ages ago you'd just have to forget it !'

'We hadn't found the grindstone then,' remarked Colin grimly. He slipped the card into his pocket, and turned his attention to rolling up the mac and brush once more. He'd decided not to remind Roy that now they were no longer the only runners in the race.

10

Question—and Answer

Wheatleigh Town Hall was a square building of grimy stone and prim, cream paint. It was separated from the High Street by an equally square and prim lawn, edged with several flowers, a ragged strip of colour that tried valiantly to cheer Colin up.

From the solitary bench beside the grass he glanced up at the clock above the doorway. Still twenty minutes to go. Desperately he fished out his sketchbook and pencil, and started on what he could see of the main road. For a while, the pencil worked swiftly ; but the shops and buses that grew on the page were unconvincing, for his mind was busy elsewhere—back at school that morning.

He realized he'd been so keyed up that it was a miracle Miss Seymour had not remarked on it. Paying any sort of attention had been mental torture, and when the prayed-for bell had rung at last, he'd escaped into the fresh air in blessed relief, feeling older and isolated from all the others chattering and skipping around him.

By the time he had reached home, his brief joy had turned to apprehension. Eating dinner had been a heroic effort, with his mouth shrunken and dry ; luckily Mum and Dad had been absorbed in Tim's latest feat of rolling on to his stomach, and his half-finished plate earned no more than a vague rebuke. At the usual time, he'd called out goodbye and set off down Sutcliff Street as though returning to school. It was only when out of sight of home that he had wavered ; the enormity of what he was doing suddenly overwhelmed him. Then he'd remembered that whatever his punishment, he at least would still be able to go away on holiday that August. Doubling back through the side-streets, he had arrived at the Town Hall with half an hour to spare.

His pencil stopped. The sketch was finished—for what it was worth ! With a grimace he scribbled in some haphazard people on the pavement, realized they were too big, and irritably slapped the book shut.

The clock said ten to two. Unable to bear much

more, he got up and walked past the flowers to the main entrance.

A black-uniformed commissionaire dubiously demanded his business, but the sight of Colin's ticket mollified him and he pointed the way up to the first floor. There was a notice at the top of the stairs, which directed Colin along a corridor to some dark double-doors ; dangling from one of its handles was a card saying *Wheatleigh and District Historical Society. Afternoon Lectures Monthly. Visitors Welcome* And taking a deep breath, he went in.

He found himself in what was really a small hall ; at the far end were two long windows reaching almost from floor to ceiling, while facing them were about twenty rows of seats, most of them empty ; only the last four or five lines were occupied, mainly by elderly people. Several of them turned and stared, making a guilty sweat prickle his cheeks ; he blinked around, searching for somewhere inconspicuous, and hurriedly made for the end of the last row, farthest from the door.

Except for the occasional swish and thud of the door admitting latecomers, there was a nerve-taxing silence. Colin tried to sit more comfortably on his chair, but it creaked too noisily, drawing curious stares at him again. He waited, tense and miserable, while the minutes dragged by.

At last a distant clock chimed two ; a side door opened, and two people made their way to the table in front of the long window. One of them, Colin was disconcerted to see, was the Reverend Greenhale ;

while the other was an alert-looking woman with neat, grey hair.

As they sat down behind the table, the faint shuffle of feet died away expectantly. And with a keen glance round the room, the parson rose to his feet.

'Ladies and gentlemen,' he declared, 'as most of you are long-standing members of our Society, you will need no introduction to our speaker, Professor Dorothy Greaves. However, there are one or two new faces amongst you today, so I must explain for their benefit that Miss Greaves was born and bred here in Wheatleigh, and has studied its history exhaustively; one result of her deep interest in the past is that she is now Head of the Modern History Department at Bristol University. I can assure you no living person could have greater knowledge on the subject of today's talk: *The Enclosures in Nineteenth-Century Wheatleigh.*' He half-turned towards the elderly woman smiling beside him. 'Ladies and gentlemen—Professor Greaves.' He sat down amid a few desultory hand-claps, and the grey-haired woman rose briskly to her feet. Colin seized his chance to shuffle farther back on to his chair.

The first part of Miss Greaves's talk covered much of what he had learnt from the Class Project: how the bread shortage in the Napoleonic Wars had given the farmers the opportunity to sell their wheat at fabulous prices, and so make great profits; and how their greed for more had made them fix their eyes on the common land belonging to the villagers, with the intention of fencing it off—*enclosing* it—to grow more wheat for themselves. In fact, despite his first determination not to miss a solitary word, Colin's attention began to wander—until all at once his ears caught the name of 'Kemp'.

'Here is part of a report on the Wheatleigh Enclosure Act of 1817,' said Miss Greaves, lifting a sheet of paper off the table and beginning to read from it. '*July 10th. The House of Commons received a request for Enclosure from the Lord of the Manor, Sir Charles Kemp. Area to be enclosed: about 2000 acres bordering the south bank of the River Thorpe—large open fields, Arable and Meadow Grounds, and also several Moors, Commons and Waste Lands.*'

She paused and took a sip of water from the glass on the table; Colin kept his eyes riveted on to her face.

'Today, of course,' commented Miss Greaves with a smile, 'most of those acres are underneath our post-war engineering factories and the Rosedale housing-estate. *July 29th. A Petition against the Enclosure was received from various Owners or Occupiers of Cottages in the parish of Wheatleigh, setting forth that they are severally entitled to Common of Pasture for their Cattle and Sheep upon the said Moors, Commons and Waste Lands; and that the Lord of the Manor lately caused part of the said Moors to be fenced in and enclosed with Pales for his own sole and separate use, without the Consent of the Petitioners, which said Pales have been since pulled down by several of the Petitioners and others.*'

She returned the paper to the table, then scanned her audience shrewdly.

'Parliament passed the Enclosure Bill six weeks later,' she observed quietly. 'And the result for the farm-workers of Wheatleigh was the same as for the rest of England. As William Cobbett remarked about the effect of these Enclosures,' she went on, referring again to her notes, '*Instead of families of small farmers with all their . . . decency of dress and of manners and . . . character, we have families of paupers, with all the improvidence . . . belonging to an irrevocable sentence of poverty for life. Mr. Curwen . . . observes that he saw somewhere in Norfolk, I believe it was, two hundred farmers worth from five to ten thousand pounds each; and exclaims " What a glorious sight ! " . . . Mr. Curwen only saw the outside of the sepulchre; if he had seen the two or three thousand half-starved labourers of these two hundred farmers, and the five or six thousand ragged wives and children of those labourers; if the farmers had brought those with them, the sight would not have been so glorious*.' She placed the paper back on the table. 'Yes, Cobbett said that in 1821 : a " sentence of poverty for life "—and that was what Sir Charles Kemp imposed on Wheatleigh's villagers when he took from them the only place they had for pasturing their few pigs and goats.'

Colin sat motionless, his mind torn between a grow-ing interest in the story for its own sake, and his self-allotted task of scrutinizing it for more clues. So far, he had drawn a blank, and continued to do so for some time, as Miss Greaves went on to describe the misery and starvation that enclosure and meagre wages had brought to the Wheatleigh of long ago : many countrymen had had to live on roots and herbs, and in 1824 three labourers were found dead of hunger on the banks of the Thorpe.

Colin's legs twined themselves tightly round those of the chair as he heard again how the labourers started to band together to demand a wage increase, along with the restoration of certain village customs that had been forced out of existence. Even so, he was quite unprepared for any reference to the church steeple, though it was by no means the helpful clue he was hoping for.

'An old copy of *The Times* describes how the villagers met Kemp and the parson in the roadway by the church,' Miss Greaves was saying steadily, 'and not only demanded higher wages, but a return to the old ways of celebrating feast-days. It seems that buns used to be thrown from the steeple and beer given away in the churchyard.' She shot a swift glance at the man beside her. 'I suspect that our Chairman is rather glad his building is no longer put to such uses.'

The audience chuckled appreciatively, while the parson smiled, his stern face melting uncomfortably.

'It was at that same meeting in 1829,' went on Miss Greaves, 'that Charles Kemp showed the nature of his mentality. *Your threats are utterly valueless*, he told the angry farm-workers, *for you cannot trust each other to be loyal. Any man of you who will come to court and give evidence against ten of the others, will obtain from me immediately five hundred pounds.* It was a cunning remark, but it happened that the labourers, half-starved and desperate though they were, had a different standard of honour from that imagined by Wheatleigh's squire and magistrate. Not one of them attempted to betray his fellows.'

A few grunts of approval came from her audience, and she took the opportunity for another sip of water. Then with a quick glance at her watch, she grasped the remaining sheaf of notes and began to describe Wheatleigh's part in the Last Labourers' Revolt.

His muscles stiff from anxiety, Colin leaned forward, concentrating on every word. But he was fated to be disappointed. True, Miss Greaves went into some detail about the firing of Kemp's manor house and his accidental death ; but it was no more than Colin had learnt at school, rather less in fact, for she made no mention of the squire's collection of silver. Colin, however, could not grumble ; in his heart, he had not expected the lecture itself to help at all, and it was during question-time afterwards that he hoped to get real results, provided his nerve held out.

Blinking nervously, Colin dragooned his wandering thoughts and focused attention once more on the precise voice of the lecturer. It was gradually taking on a rounding-off tone, and narrowing his eyes against the brightness from the windows, he saw she had reached the end of her notes.

' Therefore, ladies and gentlemen,' Miss Greaves was saying with a smile, ' whenever I return to this, my home town, and see new housing-estates being built beside the Thorpe, I am almost tempted to believe there is such a thing as poetic justice : for the common land which Charles Kemp had taken from the villagers by means of the 1817 Enclosure Act now holds the homes of scores of their descendants ; while the site of his proud manor house is today no more than a brick-strewn wilderness.'

As she sat down, the audience clapped heartily. There was a sudden buzz of comment and a stretching of backs, while the parson exchanged a few words with her. Colin joined in the applause ; he hadn't understood some of the longer words, but it had been interesting, just the same ; besides, doing what every one else was doing attracted less attention.

After replacing his spectacles, the parson stood up.

' On behalf of everyone present, I must thank Professor Greaves for her talk, which I am sure you will agree was extremely informative and stimulating,' he declared. ' We will now follow our usual practice, and have questions. There must be many of you eager to pick the brains of someone so knowledgeable concerning the history of our small town. May I have the first question, please ? '

There was an awkward pause. Colin had the feeling that the members of the audience were staring rigidly at the windows, while somehow managing to eye their neighbours furtively at the same time. His palms felt strangely sticky. He wouldn't put his own question yet—better wait to see how it's done, he told himself.

' The first question, please,' repeated the clergyman briskly.

At length, with a nervous cough, an elderly lady rose

stiffly to her feet and gripped the back of the chair in front. Speaking rather hesitantly, she asked Miss Greaves's opinion on to what extent the Enclosures had caused the death of certain rural crafts, weaving, basketry, and so forth. And the moment the sprightly lecturer began to reply, the room began gradually to thaw out ; cramped legs were straightened, arms folded more comfortably, and the chairs creaked more naturally.

After that, other members of the audience appeared to find their courage. Five more questions were put, all by people past middle age. Miss Greaves answered them all wittily and concisely, using equal charm even on those questions which strayed somewhat from the point. One old gentleman, referring to the custom of throwing buns from the church steeple, actually asked whether that had been the same spire as today's. In her reply she explained what Colin, for one, already knew : having been rebuilt in 1934, it was *not* the same steeple ; although if the gentleman was disturbed at this architectural break with the past, he could take comfort in the fact that in view of its uniqueness, the ancient circular weather-vane had been transferred as a matter of course on to the new spire, thus preserving some slight link with the town's defunct wheat-industry.

Then the parson himself stood up, and glanced pointedly at his watch.

' Ladies and gentlemen,' he announced, ' we have precisely ten minutes left ; our room-booking expires at four o'clock. May I have the last question from you ? '

Colin swallowed hard as those gimlet eyes roved inquiringly round the room. His mouth was suddenly parched; his limbs numb, no longer a part of him. Any second his chance would be gone—yet somehow the realization only paralysed him the more.

'Come now,' uttered the clergyman persuasively. 'Surely we are not so well informed on Wheatleigh's past as all that? One more question to close the meeting.'

The room was hushed. Colin's heart pummelled in torment.

'For the last time,' warned the parson, frowning at his watch. Then he added cajolingly, 'It needn't be restricted to the Enclosures—any aspect of local history will suit Miss Greaves, I'm sure!'

It was then that from the corner of his eye Colin saw an arm being raised at the far side of the room, to attract the Chairman's attention; and in a flood of fear he somehow found the strength to force up his own hand and flutter it desperately.

'Ah! That's more like it,' declared the clergyman impassively. 'This is what usually happens, of course. People keep their questions till the very end, and then there's not enough time for them all.' With the faintest of smiles, he turned to the grey-haired woman beside him. 'Miss Greaves, there are two questioners awaiting your pleasure. Which shall it be?'

'I'm making no enemies here today,' chuckled the lecturer, protestingly. 'You're the Chairman: you must play executioner.'

The Reverend James Greenhale looked wryly from one raised hand to the other. Colin felt physically sick.

'As we are an historical society,' announced the parson humorously, 'we'll let the ages decide. All the questions so far have come from elderly members, so we must now let the younger generation take the floor. Since this is his first attendance, and since I know he is fond of church history, I am sure you will forgive me for ruling in favour of our schoolboy.'

He looked directly at Colin, and nodded.

His brain a chaos of relief and fright, Colin struggled to his feet. As if from afar, he heard the scrape of chairs as the audience manoeuvred to eye him curiously. He felt his upper lip quivering, beyond his control.

'This—this has got nothing to do with—with your talk, Miss,' he began, the huskiness in his voice almost unnerving him. He swallowed hurriedly, and rushed on : 'But my pal and me—we've just come across an old grindstone. It's in the yard where his uncle works. And it's got a date carved on it : 1823. And—and we wondered if you'd know where it came from, Miss.'

It had tumbled out somewhat clearer than he'd expected ; funny how a tight corner conjured up the right words. He was just sinking gratefully back on to his chair, when Miss Greaves called pleasantly, 'What yard was this, sonny ? A private garden, you mean ?'

Colin shook his head, battling with a fresh surge of panic. 'No, Miss. It was in Rimmington's—you know, the printers right next the river.'

'Ah yes, of course ! ' she murmured, nodding her

head vigorously. Then with a quick glance at her watch, she stood up. 'I shall have to be brief—the caretaker will be evicting us in three minutes! Well then, at first sight, our young friend seems to have unearthed something of a riddle. Rimmington's, who've been printing placards, leaflets and paper-carriers ever since I was a little girl, have an 1823 grindstone on their premises! A puzzle indeed, ladies and gentlemen. Yet I think our Chairman will agree with me when I say the solution is extremely simple.' Colin noticed the parson smile dryly and start polishing his spectacles. 'You see, that large building beside the Thorpe hasn't always been Rimmington's. I don't know exactly when they moved in, but whenever it was, they were bound to have a great deal of alteration to make inside.'

Into Colin's head flashed a picture of the weed-tangled rubble-heap Roy and he had sweated over. He leaned forward intently, his eyes fastened on the lecturer's lips.

'Why do I know this? you might ask,' she continued. 'Well—have you ever wondered why that building has no windows facing the river? Or why that same wall drops sheer into the water? Both these facts have a simple explanation; which is that until this century that wall bore an enormous, wooden water-wheel, nearly as huge as the "Big Wheel" at our Whitsun fair!' She gave Colin a broad smile, and swept up her notes from the table. 'You see, in Kemp's time our quiet little river helped to grind out each year's harvest of good Wheatleigh corn : for Rimmington's was a flour-mill—and our young friend there must have found one of its discarded grindstones ! '

As she sat down amid a ripple of applause, Colin's mind whirled. Thunderstruck, he remembered the Tight-rope—then realized ruefully how obvious the explanation had been, all the time.

He could do no more than half-listen to the rest of the proceedings. The Reverend James Greenhale said something about thanking their speaker, and outlined their Society's plans for the month of June ; then the Town Hall caretaker poked his head round the door, and all at once the meeting was over.

Leaving the platform, Miss Greaves began to shake hands and exchange greetings with old friends in the audience ; the granite-faced clergyman, however, appeared to be making his way purposefully through the throng, and Colin wormed promptly for the doorway. He had an idea that the Reverend James Greenhale would ask some awkward questions if given the chance —and he'd be in quite enough trouble, as it was, when they found he'd skipped school. He wasn't quite certain whether his latest discovery would turn out to be worth it ; anyhow, it should at least put them a step ahead of Brooksbank.

He flitted through the double-doors, and out into the dim corridor leading to the top of the stairs. Several members of the Society were already sauntering along, arguing in a leisurely fashion over the Enclosures ; he hurried past them self-consciously, and thankfully joined the busier stream clattering briskly down the stairs.

He was almost at the bottom, his mind delving hope-fully into Kemp's verse once more, when all at once he realized there was someone walking with him. It was a boy, a boy his own size, who was deliberately keeping in step. Colin turned his head to glare—and then gasped.

'Hullo, Trant!' grinned his chubby-faced com-panion. 'Read any good poems lately? Anyway—thanks for telling us all about that grindstone!'

And before Colin could collect his wits, Victor Brooksbank had shot out of the main door and across the lawn, and had vanished into the High Street crowds.

11

A Matter of Spelling

Wednesday brought the inevitable punishment. Mr Hull always caned boys who played truant, and Colin neither expected nor received anything different. He had to explain where he had been, and over the telephone the vicar of St Mary's duly confirmed his story ; the parson added, however, that he hadn't realized his invitation would mean missing an afternoon's school, and perhaps this was why the Headmaster gave Colin one stroke instead of the usual two.

For his homework that week Colin had to write a four-page essay explaining what he had learnt at the lecture. Remembering his questions about nineteenth-century Wheatleigh and the church, Miss Seymour guessed there was more behind his truancy than a sudden passion for history. The composition might reveal his motive.

Things were worse at home. Mr Hull sent a letter to Colin's mother and father, and their earnest attempts to be understanding and patient made something shrivel inside him. As he couldn't tell them the true reason, he had to pretend he'd gone on a sudden stupid impulse ; and the half-puzzled way in which they believed him made him ashamed.

It took two whole evenings to write Miss Seymour's essay; he worked at it after tea in his bedroom, above the drone of the television in the living-room.

Having to put everything into writing made it easier to take stock; and the more he wrote and pondered, the more he realized how little he had gained. The lecture itself had supplied no fresh clues, a disappointment which he had half-expected; much more disheartening was the fact that discovering the origin of the grindstone had brought them no nearer solving Kemp's riddle. How could you marry it to the steeple, Colin thought in disgust, unless you played some fantastic kind of hoop-la?

It was only as the essay grew that he began to appreciate that Roy and he were now actually in a *worse* position. Brooksbank had the snuff-box lid—that seemed certain after what he'd said on the Town Hall stairs. And now he knew as much as they did about the grindstone.

All through that week the memory of Brooksbank made Colin hot with anger. *He* of course had not got into trouble for attending the lecture instead of school; he had brought a note the day before, saying his father wanted to take him on a cultural outing. Brooksbank's father, decided Colin sourly as he worked on the essay, would probably swear his son had two wooden legs, if Carrot-hair asked him to. He started to wonder whether Brooksbank had made any headway with the verse. It would be just their luck if he had.

With such thoughts irritating him, it wasn't surprising

that the essay dragged, and was not handed in till Friday afternoon. But Saturday morning brought freedom, and the chance to make at least some headway in another direction.

On their arrival at the Old Field, he enlisted Roy to fill his water-jar at the stream, then settled himself determinedly on the grassy hillock. Opening his sketch-book, he pencilled out the main landmarks, so familiar by now that he could have drawn them with his eyes closed—not that he tried, for with luck this would turn out to be the version he'd enter for the Competition. While Roy watched moodily, he took up his brush and set to in earnest.

' Waste of a fine morning,' pronounced the older boy at length, sprawling himself out on the slope.

Colin delicately stroked in the marrow-green hue of the hawthorns.

' Was hoping we'd dam the stream today,' continued Roy meaningly.

' I know,' grunted Colin, ' but the Competition closes in under two weeks, and it might be raining next weekend.' Now, if he watered down the green, he'd make those trees look their proper distance.

' All the more reason for not wasting this one,' muttered Roy irritably, tugging out a handful of grass-stems.

Colin finished off the hawthorns, then tried to steer the conversation on to smoother ground. ' Had any more ideas about the verse yet ? '

His thin face grimacing, Roy shook his head.

'Though I still think we should try what I said last night,' he declared forcefully.

Colin was considering the sunlight on Rimmington's peaked roof; it was quite tricky—more silvery than grey; and he must take care not to forget the shadowy parts near the eaves. Mixing the colour in his paint-box lid, he replied, 'You mean your notion that the thing's in some sort of code?'

'Sure,' replied Roy. 'Doesn't make sense as it is, does it?'

'Not yet, anyway,' said Colin reservedly.

'Not yet, he says!' jeered Roy, sitting up perkily. '*Marry the steeple to yonder grindstone:* the only way that'll ever make sense is by changing the letters. Maybe A stands for Z, and B for Y, and so on.'

'We tried that and it didn't work,' pointed out Colin calmly.

'But some other code might,' rejoined Roy. 'Why not A for D, B for E, like that? Must be scores of ways we could try out.'

Colin started to work the grey evenly over the roof.

'If it was in code,' he remarked wearily, 'it wouldn't have proper words in, would it? It'd be just a row of jumbled letters. But it's in perfect English!'

'Old Hully says perfect English always makes sense,' retorted Roy facetiously. 'That poem doesn't!'

'You know very well what I mean,' insisted Colin. 'If it was in code, it'd say something like K, H, O, R, U —all jumbled letters, not making any sense. But it's in real words. All that's wrong is we just haven't seen what Kemp was driving at yet.'

Roy flopped back disgruntled on to the grass.

'What makes you think we ever will?' he growled cynically.

Colin made no reply. He was brushing some black into the lower edge of the roof before the grey paint dried out.

The new colour matched the real one quite creditably; it would do very well for the steeple slates too, he judged. He rinsed out his brush, and began mixing it in the paint-box lid.

'Heard the latest about Brooksbank?' said Roy abruptly, clasping slim hands beneath his head.

'What about him?'

'Boy in my class has seen him popping into the reference library a couple of evenings.'

Colin carried on thoughtfully with the steeple. The reference library contained those books too rare or valuable to be lent out; it also contained a collection of historic documents, letters and maps concerning Wheatleigh's past.

'If Miss Seymour knew, she'd probably faint,' he commented dryly. 'He never does a stroke during history. All the same, it's not a bad idea of his,' he admitted slowly. 'There *might* be something there—about Kemp, or the grindstone.'

He finished off the spire, then with the tip of his brush, painstakingly outlined the ancient, round weather-vane on its peak. It would be fatal to let Brooksbank steal a march on them like that, he decided.

'I might as well look in there myself on Monday evening,' he remarked.

Roy only grunted; and a few minutes later, got morosely to his feet and strolled back to amuse himself in the hut. Colin was left to complete his painting in peace.

What happened that Monday morning, however, made any visit to the library quite unnecessary.

Colin was just leaving the classroom at playtime, when Miss Seymour called him back. She had marked his essay over the weekend, and while the slowest children were finishing their milks, began to go through with him all her red-ink corrections.

Colin was more interested in escaping into the yard than in his grammar and spelling mistakes ; it had been set as his homework, he'd done it, and that was that ; such was his attitude. He hardly listened to her scrupulous explanations, just nodded or grunted in the right places.

It was the neat red ring around a word on the third sheet which arrested his attention.

Miss Seymour was about to turn the page and finish off quickly, for the milk monitors had by now removed the empty crate, when Colin's puzzlement made him point hesitantly.

' What—what's wrong with that, Miss ? ' he stammered. Surely *she*'d made a mistake there ?

' For goodness' sake, Colin ! ' said the teacher in sudden exasperation, as she realized she'd shortened her tea-break to no purpose. ' I've explained it just this minute ! You've been standing there in a dream. I'm wasting no more time on you : you'll look that up in your dictionary before you go out to play, and you'll tell me what's wrong with it straight afterwards.'

She handed him the essay and hurried out to enjoy her cup of tea during the few minutes of play that remained.

More intrigued than resentful, Colin unearthed his dictionary from the tumble of books in his desk and flipped through the pages.

Sacred . . . Saltpetre . . . Schooner . . .

Almost there. He halted the falling pages and ran his eye carefully down the column.

Setter . . . Severe . . . Yes, here it was : ' *Sew*—Verb. Fasten material etc. by passing thread again and again through holes made with threaded needle.'

Colin read it slowly twice. Then, slightly puzzled and only half-convinced, he decided to look up something else.

In his essay he had written : ' In 1817 the squire of Wheatleigh took over the common used by the villagers. He surrounded it with a fence, called an Enclosure. He wanted to sew extra wheat there, because selling corn for high prices made farmers very rich in those days.'

At the time he had been positive that ' sew ' was the correct word ; anyway, he would soon know. Finding the page he wanted, he slid his finger down the print.

There it was. ' *Sow*—Verb. Scatter seed on or in the earth for purpose of growth.'

He grimaced at himself disgustedly. It reminded him of the occasion in the village school when he'd muddled ' angel ' and ' angle ' ; he'd been just as sure then that he knew which was which.

Suddenly he paused, his desk lid half-closed. He had a strange feeling that this time things were different. He seemed to recall quite recently reading something which had mentioned *sowing*—with a needle.

And as he remembered where, the desk lid slipped from his startled fingers.

12

The Riddle Solved

' But what's the point ? '

With a puzzled frown, Roy pushed the black hair from his forehead, then perched on the oil-drum.

' For heaven's sake ! ' exploded Colin, raising his eyes imploringly to the roofing-felt ; Roy sometimes required the patience of a saint. Breathing deeply, he pulled the corrugated iron shut behind them and thumped himself down on the apple-box.

' Remember the last two lines ? ' he rapped. ' *With threaded needle is silver sown ?* '

It was the other's turn to become exasperated. ' My name's not Bird-brain, you know,' he snorted.

' Then listen,' said Colin. ' We thought it meant Kemp had sewn the silver up in something, didn't we ? '

' Like in his saddle,' declared the older boy firmly.

Colin drew another deep breath. ' Well, don't you see what I've been driving at, all the way here ? Kemp didn't sew it inside anything—it wasn't that kind of sewing ; it was the other sort, like sowing seeds. Kemp's been saying all along that he'd *buried* the silver ! '

Roy stared. For one long moment he did not move, as if his back had frozen to the old wall behind him. Then his muscles relaxed, and he pouted ruefully.

'All right—you win,' he declared, hitching himself forward. 'What now?'

'So now,' went on Colin ardently, 'we want ideas on where he was most likely to bury it.'

Roy got slowly to his feet. Absent-mindedly he began to rip loose splinters from the edge of the packing-case. For a minute, nobody spoke.

'He talks about the steeple,' muttered Roy at length. 'It could be somewhere near that—the churchyard, say.'

'How about the grindstone?' suggested Colin, cupping his head in his hands and studying the cracked linoleum at his feet. 'He might've buried it in Rimmington's yard, I suppose.' But there wasn't much conviction in his voice.

'Say—I know!' All at once Roy flicked the splinters into a corner, his eyes gleaming. 'What about his own grounds?'

'Here? The Old Field?' Colin frowned doubtfully.

'Why not? Safer for him than anywhere else. Think how easy he could have slipped out one night and buried it in his garden; that way he'd be sure the villagers wouldn't spot him, and he'd be able to keep an eye on the place afterwards.'

It was the best suggestion so far. Colin nodded reluctantly. Then he shrugged.

'Even then, we're no nearer,' he growled. 'Not unless we aim to pass the next few years digging up the Old Field.'

Roy slumped slowly on to the edge of the packing-case. They regarded each other in silence.

'If you'd buried something in a big plot of land,' muttered Roy vaguely, as if groping in the dark, ' you'd have to mark the spot, wouldn't you ? Like remembering it was so many paces from a certain tree.'

' *That's it !* ' whooped Colin. He leapt to his feet. His fists were clenched, his eyes sparkled like dark crystals.

' Don't you see ? ' he cried, as Roy stared dumbly. ' What you just said : Kemp *did* mark the spot ! Like pirates are supposed to ! '

For an instant Roy thought his friend had lost his senses.

' What the devil have pirates got to do with it ? ' he exploded.

' Think of *Treasure Island* ! ' urged Colin, trying to contain himself. ' The instructions on the back of the map ! To find the treasure, they had to get certain things in line : one was a tall tree, and another was Skeleton Island ; another landmark was one of the hills.'

All at once Roy saw. He looked at Colin with wild, excited eyes.

' And Kemp's landmarks were the steeple—and the grindstone ! ' he whispered.

Swallowing hard, Colin nodded.

' *Marry the steeple to yonder grindstone,*' he quoted. ' Remember we said " Marry " used to mean " unite " ? So we've got to get the steeple in line with the grindstone——'

He stopped abruptly.

' But you can't see the grindstone from here,' protested Roy uncertainly. ' So how will——'

Then he saw that Colin already knew.

Sinking back on to the box, the younger boy sighed ; he might've known there'd be a snag. Of course, you could see the *steeple* all right from almost anywhere on the Field ; he'd painted it enough times since February to know that. Into his mind drifted the familiar picture—the javelin-blade of the spire piercing the blue-grey sky, while on the other side of the page, deliberately balancing the skyline, rose the broad, squatter peak of Rimmington's, the old water-mill.

And then everything fell into place.

' Of course ! ' he blurted hoarsely. ' It's—it's the buildings where they belong that count : Unite the steeple-building to the grindstone-building ! '

Roy stared dumbly.

' Don't you see ? ' crowed Colin, springing up in jubilation. ' We get the two roofs in line ! '

Roy nodded doubtfully. ' I—I suppose it could mean that,' he muttered at last. Then he added slowly, ' But what about the " threaded needle " bit ? If it's not the kind of sewing we thought it was——'

' I think I know that too, now,' croaked Colin excitedly, heaving the corrugated iron to one side. ' Come on—I'll show you ! '

Swiftly he led Roy up out of the hollow and past the hawthorns. The evening sun warmed his cheek and he broke into a run, as if it had kindled some spark inside him. More uncertainly, the older boy followed, past the yellow gorse, up the clay slope, then round the flowering blackberry clumps ; this was their usual route to the sketching hillock, and Roy was slightly surprised to see Colin veer off suddenly towards the long, flat ridge nearer the fence.

Trotting breathlessly up its grassy slope, they halted beneath the willow tree standing sturdily at the crest's end. Colin nodded in the direction of the river.

' See how they're dead in line from here ? ' he panted.

On the horizon, the church spire appeared to sprout upwards from the tip of Rimmington's roof.

' 's matter of fact, that's the reason I didn't paint from this place,' added Colin, 'though I tried it to begin with. Now, have a look at the top of the steeple.'

Roy's eyes narrowed as they peered at the distant, dusk-blue sky. Within his iron circle, the farmer with his scythe pointed meaninglessly north-west, a relic of last Saturday's winds.

' What about it ? ' grunted Roy ; he'd had enough of weather-vanes from the Reverend James Greenhale.

' Notice the hoop all the way round ? ' said Colin eagerly. ' Then pretend it's the eye of a needle ! '

Wrinkling his brows perplexedly, Roy stared again at the steeple ; suddenly he understood.

' I get it ! ' he exclaimed. ' That's Kemp's needle ; and the mill roof is the thread ! '

' Right first time,' grinned Colin. He began to move off along the crest of the ridge. ' Come on, before it's too dark : there'll only be one place where Rimmington's roof looks as if it's threading through that circle.

That is, if we've guessed right,' he couldn't help adding prudently.

Leaving the shelter of the willow tree, they set off side by side.

The long ridge pointed so directly towards the two landmarks that Colin became more than ever convinced that at some time or other it must have been deliberately shaped ; perhaps it had been an embankment of flowers or a broad terrace in the squire's grounds. Had it been made as a special marker for the buried silver ; or had Charles Kemp merely made use of something laid down by the gardeners of his father, Leonard, or of his grandfather, Sir Grenfell ? Colin realized that he would probably never know.

Keeping their eyes glued to the horizon, the two boys neared the end of the ridge ; and the further they advanced, the more the peak of the old water-mill mounted up the spire, creeping ever nearer to the round eye of the weather-vane . . .

Through the cooling air came the drone of traffic burrowing among the distant streets, and the faint hum of late-shift machinery in the nearby factories. But on the Old Field all was silent and still, except for the dry grasses crackling beneath their feet.

Suddenly the ground sloped downward ; they had reached the ridge's end. Scrambling warily down the steep bank, they found themselves on the lip of a hollow overgrown with dockweed. Colin was about to plough through, when he realized that their sudden drop could have taken the landmarks out of sight.

He paused and looked anxiously at the horizon.

And a stream of fire ran through his veins.

' We're there ! ' he breathed. ' We're standing on it, now ! '

It was true. From the edge of the hollow, Rimmington's roof completely masked the church spire ; and Roy's searching eyes made out the hoop of the weathervane encircling its very tip.

For some moments neither of them moved.

It was Roy who spoke first.

' Tomorrow night, then,' he said.

Colin slept badly. His bed seemed hot, and he twisted restlessly until well past midnight. Then, though his muscles rested, his seething mind would not ; and it was only when daylight came filtering through the bedroom curtains that his eyes crept shut at last.

It was no wonder that the following day at school, they smarted continually, and when Miss Seymour spotted the dark patches beneath them, she knew the kind of work to expect from him that day. Partly through his bad night, partly through excitement, he did exercises wrongly which normally he would have taken in his stride, and as the day wore on, he became ever more agitated and peevish. Would four o'clock *never* come ?

Dinner-time was a mixed blessing, a tantalizing escape that gave them barely enough minutes to take a shovel and a spade to the Old Field and deposit them at the hut. Unable to resist a quick look at the new-found hollow, they arrived back at school three minutes late. Colin felt that their ticking-off was well worth it.

During the Art lesson he noticed that Brooksbank was still away, though whether he was genuinely ill, or enjoying another of his father's 'cultural outings', Colin had no idea. Perhaps he was still ferreting in the library, Colin told himself with a chuckle.

Probably due to an interesting Art lesson, four o'clock arrived in the end with surprising speed. His heart suddenly hammering, Colin found himself putting away his work and tidying up ; a moment later class was dismissed.

He met Roy at the end of the road.

In five breathless minutes they reached the housing-estate leading to the factories. Then, some of their pent-up energy abated, they slowed into a jerky walk.

'We—we don't want to get there tired out,' advised Colin.

Roy snorted derisively, too keyed up for such tactical niceties ; but he followed Colin's lead.

They strode swiftly through the remaining streets, until the old fence was at last in sight ; then even Colin could not control the quickening of his step. They tumbled through the hole, after no more than a cursory glance to see whether anyone was looking.

'Spade and shovel first !' cried Roy, leading the way over the thick grass.

They sped past the sketching hillock, and then leapt the meandering stream ; from there it was a switch-back race over banks and ditches, till the clay slope was reached. They arrived at the bottom in one reckless slither ; and then began the familiar last sprint through the scattered bushes and hazels.

It was just as he was rounding the last of the brambles that Roy fell.

Something was protruding from the tangled boughs, almost hidden by the tall grass. He saw it the instant before it caught his ankle and pitched him headlong to the ground.

'You all right ?' panted Colin anxiously, arriving in time to help him up.

There was a smear of blood on the taller boy's cheek where it had grazed a half-buried brick ; otherwise, the dense grass and weeds seemed to have broken his fall. He clutched a handkerchief to his sore face.

'Too much of a crazy rush,' he growled ruefully. He felt his knees tenderly, while Colin picked up the penknife and cigarette cards that had shot from his pocket, and handed them back.

'Thanks,' grunted Roy. Then he frowned.

'Tripped over something back there,' he murmured. 'For a sec it looked just like——. Better have a look, case I do it again on the way back !' he added with a lop-sided grin.

Reluctantly Colin went back with him, but had no real idea of where to look. It was Roy who discovered it.

Projecting from the dark-green nether leaves, and half-hidden among rising buttercups and ragged robin, was a long wooden handle.

'Some fool's wanted to get rid of it,' snorted Roy angrily, 'and just slung it in here any old how. Might've broken my neck!'

With one savage heave, he tugged it out—and then gasped.

Colin looked too. And his heart turned to ice.

It was the spade they had put in the hut that dinner-time.

Its face was heavily streaked with clay; its shoulder bore a crust of soil and grass, where someone had scraped his soles on it.

As if in a nightmare, Colin found himself scrambling after Roy. The older boy was running at madman's pace towards the ridge. Through the labyrinth of thorny bramble and gorse they sped, up the steep clay bank to the stream once more, jumping the ditches in their path like frightened deer. Roy's long legs drew him steadily ahead; half a dozen times Colin slithered and stumbled.

Scrambling from one of the gullies, sobbing for breath, he suddenly saw the end of the ridge. Roy was just lurching up to the neat hollow at its foot.

His heart almost bursting, Colin covered the last few yards; then, standing beside Roy, he gazed down the shallow slope.

The spot they had marked out the night before had gone. In its stead gaped a broad hole, three or four feet deep. The coarse, green dock leaves round its lip lay trampled and half-smothered beneath a mound of earth and stones.

13

The Truth

They found Brooksbank in the Rosedale Recreation Park, near his home.

He was sitting moodily on one of the swings, his toes scraping the dust ; judging by the droop of his lips, his thoughts were not inspiring.

He was so preoccupied that he didn't notice them till it was almost too late. Then his flabby cheeks paled ; his chest heaved sharply ; and the next instant the swing was flying crazily backwards, as he hurled himself towards the nearest gate.

For all his chubbiness he could move quickly, and the sting of fear made him quicker still. But the passion with which Roy sped forward that night would have cornered an eel.

He tore over the grass almost before Colin had drawn breath ; seeing he would never make the gates in time, Brooksbank swerved desperately for cover among the nearby trees, but Roy threw himself at his heels and brought him down inside a dozen paces.

When Colin arrived he was sitting on Brooksbank's chest. The captive was wriggling like a hooked fish, whining and sobbing, but he wisely went limp as soon as Colin took a firm grip of his legs.

'Where've you put Kemp's silver?' panted Roy.

Brooksbank's body shook with a fresh outburst of crying.

'Snivelling won't help you,' said Colin definitely; he tightened his grasp of the other's ankles. 'You just tell us what you've done with the silver.'

'D—don't know what you mean,' stuttered Brooksbank. 'Haven't heard of any—any silver.'

'Very funny, I'm sure,' muttered Colin grimly. 'Pity we don't believe you. You know what we mean, all right. You pinched Kemp's lid from my coat-pocket for one thing, didn't you? And you went to that lecture for another——'

'And today you pinched that spade from the hut,' snapped Roy, 'and dug up the silver with it. Where've you put it?'

'Honest—I don't know what you're talking about,' pleaded Brooksbank, staring up at them with tearful eyes. 'I—I haven't even been near the Old Field today!'

'That's peculiar,' declared Colin. 'You've got its clay all over your shoes and half-way up your socks.'

'Nice set of blisters on his hands too,' grunted Roy sourly. 'Suppose he'll tell us he got 'em from reading reference books! Come on, Brooksbank; we've played around long enough. Where's Kemp's silver?'

Brooksbank lay still and silent; the short truce had brought back some of his normal nerve and bluster, stopping his tears.

'What if I have got clay on my shoes, and blisters

142

on my hands?' he muttered at last. 'What if I did do a bit of digging at the Old Field today? It's none of your business.'

The two boys looked down at him unbelievingly for one long minute. Then Roy's eyes blazed, and he got to his feet. He signed to Colin, and they made Brooksbank stand up.

'It's our business, right enough,' said Roy thickly. '*We* found the snuff-box lid, and *we* found the grind-stone. If it wasn't for us, you'd never have dug up anything!'

Brooksbank opened his mouth as if to protest, then caught the dangerous glint in Roy's eye.

'First of all,' said Colin deliberately, 'you're going to tell us how you knew where to dig, and then what you've done with the silver.'

Each of them gripping an arm, they regarded him steadily and waited. He glanced around furtively, but a few girls on the tennis court were the only people in sight.

'I—I'm not telling you anything,' he blurted at length, with a sudden show of bravado.

'All right,' said Roy, deathly calm. 'Who's it going to be, then?'

Brooksbank looked up, his ginger hair flopping nervously.

'W—what do you mean?'

'Which of us're you going to fight?' explained Colin simply.

There was a moment's silence. The chubby boy's

gaze flickered from side to side ; Colin saw the tiny nerve twitching in his nether lip.

All at once Brooksbank jerked into action. He kicked out viciously at Roy's ankle, catching the tall boy by surprise ; then, wrenching one arm free, he swung it straight for Colin's face. Colin ducked instinctively, and Brooksbank was able to tear loose his other hand and jab it savagely into his ribs.

A wave of pain shot up from Colin's stomach, and he saw, as if through a mist, that he'd left Brooksbank a clear run to the gate.

He remembered flinging himself forward desperately as that sheaf of ginger hair flashed past. For one agonizing instant he clawed at Brooksbank's shoulders ; then felt a wave of exultation as his grip held and the other overbalanced and fell.

Unable to stop himself, Colin toppled too. The next instant he found himself striving frantically to get on top, as they writhed together on the grass.

' It's up to you, Colin ! '

Roy's cry reached him just as Brooksbank's free hand started to batter his chest ; squirming wildly to one side, he tried to beat the other off, but Brooksbank's weight gave him the upper hand and made it just about impossible.

Time and again those sickening blows stabbed into his ribs, bringing that mist before his eyes once more. Time and again he twisted over, trying to grab those flailing fists. Once as they rolled together, punching indiscriminately, Colin caught a glimpse of Roy's face ;

then it was swiftly blotted out as Brooksbank struggled
again on top.

'Come on, Colin ! *Come on !* '

The agony in Roy's voice roused him to a supreme
effort. Summoning all his remaining strength, he
managed to grab one of those pummelling fists and
hang on. With his other hand he clung on to Brooksbank's shoulder and tried to drag him down.

His opponent's free fist beat a savage tattoo on the
side of his head. Gritting his teeth, Colin pulled, with
every ounce of strength he possessed. Still Brooksbank
did not fall, and the blows became like hammers on
his skull. Through the pain, Colin realized it was now
or never ; and if he should lose his grip . . .

Suddenly he squirmed to one side and heaved ;
taken by surprise, Brooksbank crashed to the ground
beside him, and in an instant Colin leapt on top.
Before the other could stir, he was pinioned beneath

Colin's knees and his ribs were receiving the same punishment he himself had meted out so freely.

The ginger-haired boy, however, was made of weaker stuff; and it was barely a couple of minutes before his eyes filled with tears and he whimpered hoarsely for Colin to stop.

'Make him promise he'll tell us what we want,' cut in Roy grimly.

Brooksbank nodded vigorously, then choked and had a bad attack of coughing. It was several moments before he again blinked up at them with glistening eyes.

'Now, how did you know where to dig?' demanded Colin. 'You didn't work it out for yourself, I'll bet!'

'I—I saw you two on the Old Field this dinner-time,' gulped Brooksbank, twisting his head uncomfortably on the grass. 'I was sort of playing behind the ridge, and you came dashing past with that spade and shovel.'

'So you hid and then watched us visit the place on our way back?' concluded Roy sourly.

Brooksbank looked away and nodded.

'So where did you put the silver?' asked Colin.

'You're—you're crushing me, Trant!' panted the other suddenly, straining for breath.

'So where did you put the silver?' repeated Colin calmly, not moving an inch.

For an instant Brooksbank stared up at the two friends with a queer look in his eye; then he grinned unpleasantly. 'There wasn't any,' he said.

They surveyed him coldly.

'Let me take over, Colin,' muttered Roy thickly. 'I'll get it out of him.'

'It's true!' declared Brooksbank, his eyes widening in alarm. 'There was nothing there—honest!'

Genuine fear sounded in his voice, but they knew him too well to be convinced. For a moment Colin hesitated, then recalled his bare-faced lies about the pencil-case. He got up and helped Roy jerk the other to his feet.

'Get behind him in case the rat tries to run for it,' ordered Roy. Without a flicker of expression, he squared up to the ashen-lipped Brooksbank. 'Now we'll see if your fists're as crooked as your tongue: put 'em up. If you win, you go free.'

Brooksbank looked desperately from one to the other; his hands stayed limply at his sides.

'L—look,' he croaked. 'I'm not fooling you now: there just wasn't anything there! I—I was digging all afternoon—it was torture. I got over four feet down; you must've seen how far——'

'Put your fists up,' warned Roy harshly. 'You'll change your tune after a few minutes.'

The other's cheeks turned the colour of putty; Colin noticed his fingers quivering fitfully.

'I'm telling you the truth, Smithson, if you'd only listen!' Brooksbank's voice shook. He swallowed, and tried to go on. 'Look, s—somehow you've worked out the wrong spot——'

With a hiss of fury, Roy thudded his fist into the other's chest. Brooksbank staggered back, tears of pain

147

and fright leaping to his eyes. Grimly Roy drew back his other fist and closed in, determined to find the truth, with bruised knuckles if necessary.

But they were never needed. As Brooksbank reeled back in terror, his knees gave from under him and he collapsed whimpering on to the grass.

'Get up!' cried Roy fiercely. 'Get up and fight!'

Brooksbank shook his head wildly; his whole body was trembling as he huddled his tear-streamed face on his arm.

'Y—you won't even—even listen!' he sobbed defiantly. 'You're just picking a fight for—for nothing.' His voice rose hysterically. 'I keep telling you, there wasn't any silver . . .'

For a moment Roy stood poised, his fists clenched hard, as he stared at the shuddering figure on the grass.

Then his hands fell loosely to his side, and slowly he looked away; and Colin saw by the dullness in his gaze that his friend had realized the truth at last.

'All right, Brooksbank,' muttered Roy. 'So there wasn't any silver.'

He turned and walked off, towards the park gates; and Colin saw that Brooksbank was not the only one with glistening cheeks.

14

End of a Dream

The last week of May trickled by. Colin sent in his entry for the *Wheatleigh Mail* Competition more through a timely prod from Miss Seymour than through anything else. Roy was picked for the school cricket team early in June. And the drizzly weather gradually gave place to warm sunshine.

It was not surprising that the two boys began to see less and less of each other. Several evenings a week Roy was either practising at the nets or playing in matches ; and his remaining nights were devoured in Rimmington's yard, helping maintain the delivery van. Rather more reluctantly Colin too became a workman, helping his father to fit shelves and cupboards in Mr Trant's new conservatory. To a casual observer, their drifting-apart could not have seemed more accidental.

Neither of them consciously planned it. They saw each other occasionally in the High Street or in the park, but there appeared little to talk about ; and as June wore on, a forced smile and a nod soon became all that passed between them at these chance meetings. The Old Field was never mentioned, much less visited.

Those first weeks of summer made Colin feel some-times as if he had moved into Wheatleigh all over again. The cramped streets, the ugly pavements, the whirring, crowding traffic—all seemed, once more, startlingly new and strange. This time however the thrill of exploring and finding out had gone, and he was left with a feeling of emptiness. Once the work in the conservatory had been completed, time hung heavily on his hands. At weekends he was glad to tackle any cupboard-clearing, potato-peeling or carpet-beating his mother cared to suggest; while as for the weekdays, what had once been the tedious routine of minding baby Tim while Mrs Trant prepared tea, soon became a welcome bridge between school and evening.

Rather to his parents' surprise, he ignored the longer hours of daylight that June brought. Apart from Roy, he had made no close friends, and unlike Cullerton, Wheatleigh had no woods or meadows to occupy him: on most evenings he stayed in doggedly, practising his sketching or watching the television.

The first Saturday in July brought news that did little to change his spirits.

It had been a wearing day in many respects. Tim, now in his fourteenth month, had begun to cut some new teeth and his whimperings made it impossible to concentrate on anything; and from ten o'clock onwards Colin, after forever getting in his harassed mother's way, found himself saddled with the job of keeping the kettle simmering to supply the constant hot drinks the baby seemed to need.

By the time Tim, worn out at last, sobbed himself to sleep that afternoon, Colin had become thoroughly irritable, what with his duties and the general upset. He mooned about the house till tea-time, getting on both his mother's and father's nerves ; he tried practising his sketching, then gave up in exasperation after ten minutes ; he tried to settle down in the living-room with first a library book and then a jigsaw. But everything he tackled gradually disintegrated into boredom.

He was sitting at the table that tea-time when his father laid his knife and fork on his empty plate, eased his chair back a little, and regarded him resolutely.

' Looking at your face, Colin,' he declared, ' anyone'd think it was you who was cutting fresh teeth today. Going to tell me what's up ? '

' Nothing's up, Dad,' he muttered awkwardly. He finished off his pie as perkily as he could, but it didn't help.

' In trouble at school ? ' said his mother sharply,

leaning over to pour out her husband's last cup of tea.

Colin shook his head vigorously.

His parents exchanged long-suffering glances. Mr Trant reached for the evening paper on the sideboard.

'Playing out with Roy tonight?' he murmured.

'Haven't been out with him for weeks,' replied Colin bleakly, obligingly falling into the trap.

'Fallen out, I suppose?' commented his mother, as she started to clear the table.

'Not really. He just keeps clear, that's all.'

Mrs Trant sighed, as if boys' ways were beyond her. She carried the first load into the kitchen, and there was silence while Mr Trant took his paper into the armchair, and Colin piled up the remaining crockery.

He was about to carry it into the kitchen, when his father looked up from his newspaper.

'Here's a bit about that Art Competition of yours.'

Colin paused in the doorway. There was an abrupt silence while Mr Trant read the rest of the column.

'Mmmm . . . Heavy odds.'

Fighting down his curiosity, Colin took the crockery in to his mother, then returned for the sugar and cruet.

'Here : you read it,' ordered his father, thrusting the paper at him.

Colin spread it out on the table. His father's thumb stabbed at a heading near the bottom.

THE WHEATLEIGH MAIL
JUNIOR ART COMPETITION

There has been a record number of entries for our Spring Painting Competition.

It is now five weeks since the closing date, and the pictures have been sorted into groups according to their content. The biggest number of children decided that their Ideal Holiday would be on a broad, sandy beach : 47 entries. The next largest group plumped for the many pleasures of a holiday camp : 33 entries. Rather surprisingly, the third biggest group picked the country-side, a sophisticated choice for under-sixteens these days : 28 entries. Different kinds of sports accounted for 25 entries, and there were 14 miscellaneous ones, such as excavating for Roman remains, attending field-courses in biology, etc. This gives a grand total of 147 paintings—beating the previous record by 18.

Our judges are now attempting the difficult task of selecting the best three. Their final verdict will be printed in our issue of 26th August. In the meantime, we should like to thank all who entered. The holiday season is almost here : may it bring an Ideal Holiday both to you and to all your friends.

Colin handed the paper back. Without a word, he cleared the sugar and cruet off the table. There would be no holiday for *his* friends, ' ideal ' or otherwise.

15

Colin Remembers

Inexorably the days passed : and the routine of errands and lessons had to be surmounted as though nothing had happened. It took a great deal to halt the world's course, Colin realized bleakly.

He slipped into bed every night half-glad another dragging day was over, and half-tormented by the thought that nothing now could turn up for Roy in time. Sometimes it was fairly easy to forget, in the classroom or at play ; but afterwards during meals or walking home, it would come back to him, like shouldering a heavy burden once more.

And then it was the last weekend in July. The Saturday morning and afternoon were spent as usual in a succession of jobs for his mother, cupboard-clearing, running to the shops, helping in the kitchen, looking after Tim.

When evening came, he was squatting on the floor of the conservatory, wiping the undercarriage of Tim's pram. 'Now Tim has the push-chair so much, love, that pram could do with a good clean,' Mrs Trant had suggested after tea, in response to his request for more jobs. 'It's stood out there since Whitsun, gathering so much dust it's just about growing whiskers.' And she had handed him a duster, rags and some metal polish without more ado.

'Whiskers' was right,' thought Colin dryly, as he threaded the duster between the spokes and broke yet another cobweb; that was the third so far. It put him in mind of all those cobwebs—not to mention germs and damp, which his mother in her spring-cleaning fervour had 'seen' in number 81 when they'd first moved in; Operation Scrubbing-from-Top-to-Bottom, which had followed, had taken the best part of a Sunday. He could remember helping his dad to shift all the furniture as clearly as though it were only a fortnight ago. He sat on his heels for a moment, and worked it out. Five months! Hard to believe, till he recalled that mum had already made packing lists for their summer holidays.

Their summer holidays: his very first trip to the seaside . . . But somehow the thought excited him no longer.

Seven days at Ilfracombe, it was going to be. It would have been a fortnight, his mother had explained, but they'd had to buy Tim the push-chair and a new cot and a fresh outfit of clothes now that he was starting to toddle. Colin snorted at the memory: money trouble again, it seemed.

Then he flushed, suddenly ashamed of himself. Even a single day at the seaside would be wonderful, for— for some people . . .

He rubbed savagely at the gleaming springs, bursting another cobweb into a hundred limp threads.

A small spider scuttled along the framework, and bobbed down the grey curve of the wheel. Colin paused, and watched. It gained the whiteness of the concrete floor, then shot on its eight piston-legs towards the nearest corner. It scuttled into the gloom behind a leg of his father's workbench, and stopped.

Colin waited. He could just see one of its bent-wire legs protruding from behind the wood, silhouetted against the yellow of the new brick wall. Then the black wire twitched, and edged itself out of sight. Colin watched, trying to guess whereabouts on the far side of the leg it might reappear ; but nothing happened, and with a shrug he turned back to his work. It had probably decided to lie low for a while, and even if it did scamper out on to the other wall, he realized, he'd hardly be able to spot it, for those bricks were the old, grey ones of the house proper.

He started to whisk the duster round the rim of one of the wheels, and then stopped. He had the strange feeling that what he'd just seen was a repetition of something else. He peered again into the table corner, where the house-wall of faded brick met the fresher stonework of the conservatory : the grey and aged beside the bright and the new.

Where had he seen that before ? The question stole quite unwanted into his mind. Not very long ago, he felt, he'd noticed something almost exactly the same.

His brow furrowed, but at first nothing came. It was only when he turned with a shrug to complete the dusting, that it leapt into his memory. It was when they had been in the churchyard of St Mary's, listening to the Reverend James Greenhale ; he remembered asking him some sort of question . . .

Of course ! The eaves of the steeple ! He'd noticed that the bricks there were a different colour from those below . . . Now, what had the parson said ? Something about the steeple having been reported as unsafe round about 1930 ; oh yes, and they'd had to rebuild it, and that Greaves lady at the history lecture had said what a good thing it was that their symbolic weather-vane had been put back afterwards. Come to think of it, if it hadn't been, Roy and he would never have solved Kemp's verse at all.

Suddenly he froze. The duster dropped from his fingers, and lay unheeded on the concrete.

A tremendous idea had come to him—as if a search-light had stabbed out and lit up a black cave.

The longer he turned it over in his mind, the surer he became ; everything might still come out right, after all, though he would need every minute there was left.

With a whoop of delight, he hurled the duster into the corner, tugged open the conservatory door, and tore out into the summer evening.

' But where are we going ? ' panted Roy querulously, as Colin led him at a stiff canter down the High Street twenty minutes later.

' Save your wind for—for running ! ' came the retort, as they pounded beside the long string of shop-windows.

Roy grunted dubiously ; he remembered other wild goose chases Colin had dragged him out upon, and saw no reason why this shouldn't turn out to be another. The evening was pleasant, however, the sky grey and cool, with orange-gilt clouds framing the setting sun, and it had been a long time since he had savoured Colin's company ; so he tried to shrug his misgivings into the background.

Colin had set a stiff pace all the way from Roy's home, and by the time they reached the bridge the older boy was relieved to halt for their customary peek at the grey Thorpe slithering past below.

'Heading for Uncle Phil's place?' he asked, seeing Colin glance at the strip of bank that led to the tall printing-works.

Colin grinned at his companion's furrowed brow, and heaved himself away from the parapet. 'Does it look like it?' he asked impudently, as he continued across the bridge and led the way into the older part of Wheatleigh.

It was when they left the broad curve of the main road that Roy knew at last the answer to his question. With a grimace he fastened his eyes on the tip of the steeple just visible above the roof-tops. Another catechism on weather-vanes, or some such topic, was the last thing he felt like facing that evening.

A few minutes later his spirits rose slightly when Colin marched past the church without stopping ; but his relief was short-lived, for they halted at the very next gateway. A small notice told him this was the vicarage.

'You can count me out,' he announced firmly, not moving an inch as Colin thrust open the iron gate.

'You'll come—and like it!' retorted Colin swiftly, grabbing his arm and tugging him down the pathway; and there was an infectious something in his voice that allayed all argument.

It was Colin who mounted the steps and rang the door-bell.

They had a short wait, then the door was opened by a middle-aged woman dressed in blue, who eyed them inquiringly.

'Please—could we see the vicar?' asked Colin.

'Is he expecting you?' she demanded.

He shook his head.

'Then what's it about?' Her suspicious tone warned Colin he was in danger of being sent packing, unless he picked his words shrewdly.

'He knows me from the local History Society,' he said politely. 'I—I'd like to ask him a question about the church, please.'

'You're a bit young to be worrying your heads about history, aren't you?' she remarked caustically; but she went back down the passage, and a minute later the Reverend James Greenhale appeared.

'I thought it must be you,' he declared grimly, fixing Colin with a cold eye. 'The boy who unearthed the grindstone, and played truant to attend Dr Greaves's lecture.'

Colin flushed; he had hoped that that might all have been forgotten.

'I hear you've another question about the church,' remarked the parson after a slight pause.

Colin tried to rally his wits.

'If it's not too much trouble, sir,' he asked politely. As the clergyman made no reply, but merely removed his spectacles and began to polish them with a corner of his handkerchief, Colin hurried on. 'You—you told me last time, sir, that the steeple had been rebuilt a long time ago——'

'In 1934,' said the parson dryly.

'Yes, sir. I—I was thinking they might have changed its size a bit, you see,' stammered Colin. Now that the moment had come, he had an overwhelming feeling that his question would seem ridiculous.

'Go on,' said the parson.

Colin took a gulp of air.

'I wondered if you'd be able to tell me how—how high it was before 1934, sir.'

Those frosty eyes narrowed suspiciously, as though trying to transfix him. For several seconds the only sound was the nervous shifting of Roy's shoes on the bottom step. At length the parson said deliberately, 'If I didn't know you of old, my lad, I'd have said you were trying to waste my time : I've pointed out to you before, architectural information of that kind can be found in the porch.'

Colin started.

'I—I hadn't thought of that, sir.'

'I gather you hadn't,' remarked the clergyman impassively. 'Good night.'

With a curt nod, he replaced his spectacles and closed the door.

Colin turned, sprang down the steps and raced up the path, his heart hammering. Roy followed him speedily enough, thankful to escape so lightly, but by now more puzzled and exasperated than ever.

'Next stop the church, I suppose?' he grunted ironically, as they reached the road and turned the way they had come.

Colin nodded.

' Mind telling me why, some time ? ' snorted Roy.

' You'll see,' muttered Colin curtly, banging open the churchyard gate and sprinting down the gravel path between the gravestones.

By the time the unwilling Roy arrived in the porchway, Colin was fervidly scanning the wooden plaque fixed to the wall. Passing over the first paragraphs about the Kemps, he concentrated on some lines near the bottom. When at last he looked up, it was with a strange, suppressed excitement on his face.

He pointed to one of the paragraphs. Roy had to crouch a little to read it.

In minute yellow letters it stated :

The sum of £1700 for the reconstruction of the steeple could have been reduced, but it was deemed perfectly safe by the architects to alter its structure so as to preserve its dominance over the many tall buildings erected nearby since the First World War. One result of this is that the present spire attains a height of 121 feet ; whereas the previous was just over four-fifths of this, being 102 feet.

Roy read this stolidly twice.

' Well ? ' he growled at length.

Colin took a deep breath. He felt hot and his heart was pounding inside his chest like a steam piston.

' Can't you see,' he said, in as even a voice as he could muster, ' that now we know how high the steeple was in Kemp's time, we can work out the *proper* place he buried his silver ? '

16

Sown—and Reaped

Darkness was dimming the sky as they collected the spade and shovel from the hut, and scrambled out of the hollow. Hurrying round the hawthorns, Colin glanced anxiously at the horizon.

Like the teeth of a great saw, the far roof-tops cut a row of black wedges from the sky ; both the broad gash of Rimmington's and the upright lance of the steeple stood out clearly.

In silent satisfaction he led the way forward, through the chest-high gorse, up the steep clay bank, past the black, formless brambles. The gathering gloom made it difficult to judge the best place for your feet, and once Colin's haste made him all but sprain his ankle.

Breathless and leg-sore they reached the foot of the long ridge, and paused beside the pit Brooksbank had dug so many weeks before. Its brown earth was already veiled beneath a fuzz of grass shoots and weeds.

From where they stood, the tip of the old mill roof fitted exactly into the steeple's circular weather-vane.

'Kemp's spire was only four-fifths as tall,' breathed Colin, 'so the right spot'll be somewhere along the ridge, I should think.'

Roy nodded mutely.

Changing his grip on the shovel, Colin climbed the grassy slope; looking back, he confirmed that the mill roof appeared to have slithered a fraction down the spire.

'Now straight on, slow and steady,' he muttered, as Roy joined him and they set off together.

The long grass whispered beneath their feet as they walked, the only sound in the stillness surrounding them. It made Roy almost believe the world outside the fence had paused to listen too. Then a flight of rooks sped homing overhead, making the sky raucous, startling and reassuring him.

After thirty paces, Colin halted and checked on the two landmarks. Rimmington's peak was much lower on the church spire, but not yet on the four-fifths mark he had fixed in his mind. He remembered his dozens of sketches; he remembered standing in the churchyard and gazing up at the spire's terrifying climb; and he knew without the least doubt that four-fifths of its total height would be half-way between the clock-face and the farmer with his scythe.

He saw Roy was looking at him expectantly, and shook his head; quite a way to go yet.

They strode on, the crest stretching ahead into the gloom, as flat and straight as a pavement. Another thirty steps and they could see the trunk of the old willow tree quite plainly.

Colin glanced over his shoulder, but knew it was no more than a formality; he hurried on, his fingers beginning to ache with the shovel's weight, and the words of Kemp's riddle beating monotonously in his mind.

> *Marry the steeple*
> *To yonder grindstone.*
> *With threaded needle*
> *Is silver sown.*

Quite a dance it had led them, he thought, almost with affection for it. And it wasn't quite over yet, going by their long trek tonight ; his shoes and socks were already soaking with dew.

All at once, it seemed, the end of the ridge appeared through the darkness and they were standing beside the willow that Colin knew of old. Beyond it, the grass sloped steeply down into a sea of dock leaves and buttercup. Colin frowned ; for once down there surely the landmarks would be out of sight ?

Slowly he turned round. And his very blood seemed to sing.

For the old mill roof had reached the exact mark he had fixed down the steeple.

Swallowing hard, he glanced at Roy. There was no mistaking the tense hope shining in his friend's eyes.

Colin nodded. ' Right here,' he whispered.

For a moment not a muscle of Roy's face moved ; then his lips cracked into an exultant grin.

As the darkness deepened, they set to work.

It seemed reasonable to suppose that Kemp would have avoided the ridge's steep sides, and used the middle of its crest. Accordingly at Colin's suggestion, they marked out a ten-foot strip running from the base of

the willow trunk back towards the ' threaded needle ' ; and Roy, muttering that the roots would be too awkward for Colin to manage, took it upon himself to dig at the tree end, leaving Colin to start at the other.

It was gruelling work. First the turf, thick and wiry, had to be cut away, then scores of pebbles and stone-chippings began to jar their blades ; Kemp's gardeners had certainly meant their embankment to last, Colin realized ruefully. After half an hour his shoulders were aching from the unaccustomed effort, and he felt the first prick of fresh blisters on his hands.

Deeper and deeper he went, gradually working in-wards towards Roy still struggling under the tree ; from what he could see of the progress there, the willow roots certainly seemed more troublesome than any stones.

The best part of an hour must have passed when, leaning on his shovel for breath, he heard the church clock strike half past ten. His parents would be getting worried by now ; nine-thirty was the latest he was ever allowed out. Still, they knew by now where to find him if they wanted.

Glancing round he realized it was quite dark ; there was no moon, and in the starlight Roy's bent, heaving figure was no more than a silhouette. The bright pin-pricks of street-lamps flickered through the leaves of the willow, making the field seem one vast black void around him.

Taking a gulp of cold air, he straightened up and threw a last glance at Roy. He watched him stab in the spade, then wriggle the handle to work it deeper. He paused, waiting for the heave of his friend's shoulders and the patter of the soil as it hit the grass.

But it never came. Roy appeared not to have moved. Puzzled, Colin realized he was still standing with one foot on the shoulder of the blade, his fingers working the handle gently.

' What's up ? ' he called. ' On strike, like me ? '

There was a moment's silence. Then Roy spoke, his voice low and forced.

' Strike's the word all right. I've hit something ! '

Scrambling over the loose earth, Colin sprang down beside him.

' Feel that,' muttered Roy.

167

There was something solid beneath the blade, which grated when Colin tried to turn it.

' Could be a stone,' he pointed out, hating himself for it and yet not daring to hope for more.

' Soon see,' said Roy gruffly.

Grasping the spade, he set to work in earnest. After a moment's hesitation, Colin dashed back for the shovel.

Two thick roots forked out from the willow trunk, and it was close between these that Roy had begun his part of the digging. By now his trench was two or three feet deep, with just enough room for the two of them to work side by side ; and, reckless of each other's feet, they started to jab their blades feverishly into the black earth that lay packed and damp at its bottom.

Within a matter of minutes, there was no doubt they were nearing something large and immovable. Then all at once, Roy's spade spooned up a huge mass of soil, and there, exposed to the stars, was an edge of tarnished metal. It was the corner of a brass box.

For a minute they just stared. There was a great lump in Colin's throat ; after so much planning and striving, he was filled with nothing but a perverse disbelief.

And then the spell was broken. A trickle of earth hissed back into the trench, its suddenness startling them from their stupor ; and with yelps of delight, they hacked the box free.

It was a huge chest, nearly as long as Roy was tall, and far too heavy for them to drag up on to the grass.

A century ago there had probably been a golden gloss on its brass, but the damp earth had long since turned its sides into ebony. As for its iron lock, that was hopelessly eaten away with rust and it shattered at a single blow from Colin's spade.

With tremulous hands they lifted the lid.

Goblets. Caskets. Vases.

Engraved salvers, plates, bowls and dishes.

And jewel-cases, crammed with lockets, necklaces and bracelets of finest filigree.

They gazed dumbly. At last Colin spoke.

'Some—something *did* turn up in time, after all.'

Roy stared, not understanding him. But it did not matter; for at that moment they heard an anxious voice calling for them from the fence.

It was Mr Trant.

17

Harvest

The summer blossomed into perfection. A fierce sun shimmered down practically throughout the rest of July and well into August. For many weeks the Old Field lay unvisited. And when, a few days after returning from Ilfracombe, Colin managed to slip at last through the iron fence, it was to find the wasteland vastly altered.

The glorious summer had done more than cook his

hands and face the colour of a walnut; it had raised
a miniature jungle of weeds and wild flowers. The
yellow-tasselled gorse and black-beaded brambles had
become rocks in a green surf, with the ridge a huge
wave, foamy with seeding dandelion and groundsel.

In some ways it didn't seem more than a few hours
since that back-breaking night; but in others it
appeared longer than a year. He remembered quite
clearly watching the constables arrive, and then being
taken in a car to the police-station with his father, Roy
and the great chest. But it was the complications
afterwards, although much nearer in time, which
seemed unreal and harder to recall.

Everything had got into the hands of grown-ups. The whole story had had to be reported to the Wheatleigh Coroner, and there was an inquest, just as if someone had died and the great chest had been a body. The solicitors eventually ruled that as there were no living heirs to Kemp's estate, the silverware was treasure trove and belonged to the Crown, and the Government would have to pay the finders the full market value.

Well over two thousand pounds, it had turned out. And with Roy's half-share, Mrs Smithson, still hardly able to believe it, had taken her family for a holiday to a quiet village on the south coast.

In sudden exhilaration Colin pulled himself together and struck out for the hut, wading through ditches thronged with giant dock leaves and scarlet-tipped ragged robin. He ploughed excitedly past new hillocks of nettle and purple thistle, and found that for once he could negotiate the steep slope to the lower part of the field without slithering ; its clay was dry and fretted with cracks. Racing to the hawthorn trees, he found them so loaded with berries that they glowed in the sun like fire.

Breathlessly he trotted down into the hollow, heaved back the iron door and tumbled into the hut.

The shelf and boxes were coated in dust, and there were half a dozen midge-spattered cobwebs to be broken before he felt himself at home once more. Then, sitting on the apple-box, with his feet propped up on the stone wall, he dragged the letter from his pocket and began to read it again, for the umpteenth time.

Dear Colin,

      Mum says it's about time I wrote back, so here goes.

Thanks for sending me the newspaper cutting. I see they went the whole hog and printed everything, right from when you found the snuff-box lid. They altered some parts though, didn't they? Somehow made it all sound cleverer than it was.

I'd have loved to see old Carrot-hair's face when you shoved the newspaper under his nose! I bet he looked as if he'd swallowed some school milk that had just gone off.

Yes, I too got a letter from the vicar. ' Congratulations on your resourcefulness,' and so on. He said he'd have to see about resigning and making me Chairman of the History Society in his place. He must have got us muddled up! Still, I suppose it was pretty good of him to write to us.

Congratulations! Third out of 147! You'll be needing a larger-size cap now. What're you going to spend the prize money on? Seeing you'd just become a millionaire, I was thinking you'd probably give them the ten bob back—then I remembered that your mum's banked most of it, as mine did.

We're all having a terrific time here. I never knew it would be so glorious! It gives you a lovely free feeling to see all that sea, and acres of sand and rocks—to be able to see for miles, instead of being shut in by rows of houses and factories.

So now you know why we're staying here for another week ! But I'll be back for when school starts.

Look after the hut.

Be seeing you,

Roy

With a slow smile, Colin folded the letter up again and returned it to his pocket. For a while he sat motionless, alone with his thoughts.

At last the church clock struck the hour, reminding him it was time to go home. He slid the door shut behind him, then strolled out across the field, the sun warm on his back. Mounting the clay slope, he picked his way back through the maze of gorse and brambles.

Between the willow ridge and the fence, he came upon the small hillock where he had spent so many hours painting. He paused ; for it was here, way back in February, that everything had begun. Just suppose Brooksbank had not taken that pencil-case . . .

Then he grinned, realizing that he knew now exactly how he would spend his ten shillings.

He reached out to the nearest bush and picked half a dozen blackberries. They were large and just at the stage of ripeness he liked. Strange to think that brambles too came from the countryside ; it just showed you that some things could put roots down anywhere.

He went on and wriggled out through the hole in the fence.

Author's Note

The general historical events referred to in this story are authentic. Beginning in 1830 in Kent, where threshing-machines were destroyed, the Last Labourers' Revolt spread rapidly as far west as Dorset, where hayricks were burnt and overseers were run out of the villages, and the farm-workers marched angrily into their nearest towns to confront the magistrates more forcibly with their demands for a living wage.

A leader known as Captain Swing is said to have issued the manifesto quoted on page 43 ; whereas the words I have put into the mouth of Charles Kemp (page 43) came from a gentleman-farmer of that period and were reported in *The Times* of 3rd January 1831. In the story I have substituted the word ' crops ' for ' hops '.

Cobbett's remarks on the part played by the Enclosure Movement in lowering the living standards of the labourers (page 112) are taken from a letter of his published in the *Political Register* of 17th March 1821.

I have used similar material in three other places :

1. The report on page 111 of the Wheatleigh villagers' vain resistance to Enclosure is taken almost word for word from the Parliamentary Preamble to the Enclosure Act of 1789 applying to Stanwell in Middlesex.

2. Kemp's attempt to divide the labourers by offering £500 to an informer is modelled on a Mr Benett

of Wiltshire, whose base offer was similarly refused.

3. The distribution of beer, and the throwing of buns from the parish-church steeple, were an annual custom before 1830 at Walden in Bucks. This was known as Bun-day and seems to have been a form of Poor-relief.

Readers interested in churches will already know that their ' biographies ' are often found on wall-plaques like the one in my story, whose wording and details are both based on those of a real church in Yorkshire.

A Coroner's inquest is the correct, compulsory procedure for treasure discovered hidden in the earth. If this is proved to have been hidden with the intention of recovery later, and if there are no heirs to claim ownership, it is then judged to be the property of the Crown. The finder is paid its full market value.

The story of treasure trove in Britain through the years makes exciting reading. In 1959 two labourers digging a trench for drains came upon 718 Saxon coins in an earthenware pot, and later received £2,700. In 1942 two men, Ford and Butcher, were ploughing virgin land when they struck a hoard of priceless silverware—ladles, spoons, dishes, goblets, all covered by a magnificent two-foot tray (this is now called the Great Dish and experts put it at over 1,500 years old). The value of their discovery amounted to £60,000.

Over the years, more than 400 finds of buried treasure have been made in Britain. I conceived the idea for this book on reading that in 1958 a schoolboy had dug up a hoard of gold sovereigns in a disused field.

E. H.